Kid Scanlan

H. C. Witwer

CHAPTER I
LAY OFF, MACDUFF!

Brains is great things to have, and many's the time I've wished I had a set of 'em in *my* head instead of just plain bone! Still they's a lot of guys which has gone through life like a yegg goes through a safe, and taken everything out of it that wasn't nailed, with nothin' in their head but hair!

A college professor gets five thousand a year, a good lightweight will grab that much a fight. A school teacher drags down fifteen a week, and the guy that looks after the boilers in the school buildin' gets thirty!

Sweet cookie!

So don't get discouraged if the pride of the family gets throwed out of school because he thinks twice two is eighteen and geography is played with nets. The chances is very bright that young Stupid will be holdin' the steerin' wheel of his own Easy Eight when the other guys, which won all the trick medals for ground and lofty learnin', will be wonderin' why a good bookkeeper never gets more than twenty-five a week. And then, if he feels he's *got* to have brains around him, now that he's grabbed the other half of the team—money—he can go downtown and buy all the brains he wants for eighteen dollars a week!

So if you're as shy on brains as a bald-headed man is of dandruff, and what's more, you *know* it, cheer up! Because you can bet the gas-bill money that you got somethin' just as good. Some trick concealed about you that'll keep you out of the bread line. The thing to do is to take an inventory of yourself and find it!

Look good—it's there somewheres!

Kid Scanlan's was hangin' from his left shoulder, and it made him enough dimes in five years to step out of the crowd and watch the others scramble from the sidelines. It was just an ordinary arm, size 36, model A, lot 768, same as we all have—but inside of it the Kid had a wallop that would make a six-inch shell look like a lover's caress!

Inside of his head the Kid had nothin'!

Scanlan went through the welterweight division about like the Marines went through Belleau Wood, and, finally, the only thing that stood between him and the title was a guy called One-Punch Ross—the champion. They agreed to fight until nature stopped the quarrel, at Goldfield, Nev. They's two things I'll never forget as long as I pay the premiums on my insurance policy, and they are the first and second rounds of that fight. That's as far as the thing went, just two short frames, but more real scrappin' was had in them few minutes than Europe will see if Ireland busts loose! Except that they was more principals, the battle of the Marne would have looked like a chorus men's frolic alongside of the Ross-Scanlan mêlée. They went at each other like peeved wildcats and the bell at the end of the first round only seemed to annoy 'em—they had to be jimmied apart. Ross opened the second round by knockin' Scanlan through the ropes into the ten-dollar boxes, but the Kid was back and in there tryin' again before the referee could find the body to start a count. After beatin' the champ from pillar to post and hittin' him with everything but the bucket, the Kid rocks him to sleep with a left swing to the jaw, just before the gong.

The crowd went crazy. I went in the hole for five thousand bucks and the Kid went in the movies!

I had been handlin' Ross before that battle, but after it I wouldn't have buried him! This guy was a ex-champion then, and I don't want no ex-nothin' around *me*—unless it's a bill.

Right after that scrap, Scanlan sent for me and made me a proposition to look after his affairs for the followin' three years, and the only time I lost in acceptin' it was caused by the ink runnin' out of my fountain pen when I was signin' the contract. In them days I had a rep for bein' able to get the money for my athletes that would make Shylock look like a free spender. Every time one of *my* boys performed for the edification of the mob, we got a elegant deposit before we put a pen to the articles and we got the balance of the dough before we pulled on a glove. I never left nothin' to chance or the other guy. That's what beat Napoleon and all them birds! Of course, they was several people here and there throughout the country which was more popular than I was on that account, but which would *you* rather, have, three cheers or three bucks?

Well, that's the way *I* figured!

About a month after Scanlan become my only visible means of support, I signed him up for ten rounds with a bird which said, "What d'ye want, hey?" when you called him Hurricane Harris, and the next day a guy comes in to see me in the little trick office I had staked myself to on Broadway. When he rapped on the door I got up on a chair and took a flash at him over the transom and seein' he looked like ready money, I let him come in. He claims his name is Edward R. Potts and that so far he's president of the Maudlin Moving Picture Company.

"I am here," he says, "to offer you a chance to make twenty thousand dollars. Do you want it?"

"Who *give* you the horse?" I asks him, playin' safe. "I got to know where this tip come from!"

"Horse?" he mutters, lookin' surprised. "I know nothing of horses!"

"Well," I tells him, "I ain't exactly a liveryman myself, but before I put any of Kid Scanlan's hard-earned money on one of them equines, I got to know more about the race than you've spilled so far! What did the trainer say?"

He was a fat, middle-aged hick that would soon be old, and he wears half a pair of glasses over one eye. He aims the thing at me and smiles.

"I'm afraid I don't understand what you're talking about!" he says. "But I fancy it's a pun of some sort! Very well, then, what *did* the trainer say?"

I walked over and laid my arm on his shoulder.

"Are you endeavorin' to spoof me?" I asks him sternly. "Or have you got me confused with Abe Levy, the vaudeville agent? Either way you're losin' time! I don't care for your stuff myself, and if that's your act, I wouldn't give you a week-end at a movie house!"

He takes off the trick eye-glass and begins to clean it with a handkerchief.

"My dear fellow!" he says. "It is plain that you do not understand the nature of my proposal. I wish to engage the services of Kid Scanlan, the present incumbent of the welterweight title. We want to make a five-reel feature, based on his rise to the championship. I am prepared to offer you first class transportation to our mammoth studios at Film City, Cal.; and twenty thousand dollars when the picture is completed! What do you say?"

"Have a cigar!" I says, when I get my breath. I throwed a handful of 'em in his lap and give the water cooler a play.

"No, thanks!" he says, layin' 'em on the desk. "I never smoke."

"Well," I tells him, "I ain't got a thing to drink in the place, you gotta be careful here, y'know! But to get back to the movie thing, what does the Kid have to do for the twenty thousand fish?"

He takes a long piece of paper from his pocket and lays it down in front of me. It looked like a chattel mortgage on Mexico, and what paragraphs didn't commence with "to wit," started off with "do hereby."

"All that Mr. Scanlan has to do," he explains, "will be told him by our director at the studios, who will produce the picture. His name is Mr. Salvatore Genaro. Kindly sign where the cross is marked!"

"Wait!" I says. "We can't take a railroad ride like that for twenty thousand, we got to have twenty-five and—"

"All right!" he butts in. "Sign only on the first line!"

"Thirty thousand, I meant to say!" I tells him, "because —"

"Certainly," he cuts me off, handin' over his fountain pen. "Don't use initials, sign your full name!"

I signed it.

"How do I know we get this money?" I asks him.

"Aha!" he answers. "How do we know that the dawn will come? My company is worth a million dollars, old chap, and that contract you have is as good as the money! Be at my office at two this afternoon and I will give you the tickets. *Adios* until then!"

And he blows out of the office.

I closed down the desk, went outside and climbed into my Foolish Four. In an hour I was up to the trainin' camp near Rye where Kid Scanlan was preparin' for his collision with Hurricane Harris. Scanlan is trainin' for the quarrel by playin' seven up with the room clerk from the Beach Hotel, and when I bust in the door he takes a look, throws the cards on the floor and makes a pass at his little pal so's I'll think he's a new sparrin' partner. I pulled him off and dragged him to one side.

"How would you like to go in the movies?" I says.

"Nothin' doin'!" the Kid tells me. "They make my eyes sore!"

"I don't mean watch 'em!" I explains. "I mean act in 'em! We're goin' out to the well known Coast this afternoon and you're gonna be a movie hero for five reels and thirty thousand bucks!"

"We don't fight Harris?" asks the Kid.

"No!" I says. "What d'ye mean *fight*! Leave that stuff for the roughnecks, we're actors now!"

We got out to Film City at the end of the week and while there wasn't no brass band to meet us at the station, there was a sad-lookin' guy with one of them buckboard things and what at one time was probably a horse. I never seen such a gloomy lookin' layout in my life; they reminded me of a rainy Sunday in Philadelphia. The driver comes up to us and, after takin' a long and searchin' look, says,

"Which one of you fellers is the pugeylist?"

"Pugilist?" I says. "What d'ye mean pugilist? We're the new leadin' men for the stock company here. Pugilist! Ha! Ha! How John Drew will laugh when I tell him that!"

He takes a piece of paper from his pocket and reads it.

"I'm lookin' for Kid Scanlan and Johnny Green," he announces. "One of 'em's supposed to be the welterweight champion, but I doubt it! I never seen him fight!"

"Well," I says, "you got a good chance to try for the title, bo, if you ain't more respectful! I'm Mr. Green and that's Kid Scanlan, the champ!"

He looks at the Kid and kinda sneers.

"All right!" he says. "Git aboard and I'll take you out to Mr. Genaro. I'll tell you now, though, that if you ain't what you claim, you got to walk back!" He takes a side glance at the Kid. "Champ, eh?" he mutters.

We climb in the buckboard and this guy turns to me and points the whip at the Kid.

"He don't look like no pugeylist to me," he goes on, like he's lookin' for a argument, "let alone a champion! Still looks is deceivin' at that. Take a crab, for instance—you'd never think from lookin' at it that you could eat it, would you? No! Git up!"

Git *up* was right, because the animal this guy had suspended between the shafts had laid right down on the ground outside the station, whilst he was talkin' to us. The noble beast got gamely to its feet at the word from Gloomy Gus, give a little shiver that rattled the harness and then turned around to see what its master had drawed from the train that mornin'. It took a good eyeful and kinda curled up its lip and sneered at us, showin' its yellow teeth in a sarcastical grin.

"Hold fast!" remarks Gloomy Gus. "It's rough country here and this horse is about to do a piece of runnin'!" He takes off his belt and whales that equine over what would a been the back on a regular horse. "Step along!" he asks it.

Well, if they had that ride at Coney Island, they'd have made a fortune with it in one summer, because as soon as Old Dobbin realized he'd been hit, he started for South Africa and tried to make it in six jumps! He folded his long skinny ears back of his neck somewheres and just simply give himself over to runnin'. We went up hills and down vales that would have broke an automobile's heart, we took corners on one leg and creeks in a jump and when I seen the Pacific Ocean loomin' up in the offing I begin to pray that the thing couldn't swim! Gloomy Gus leans over and yells in my ear, "Some horse, eh?"

"Is that what it is?" I hollers back.

"Well, he's tryin' all right. He's what you could call a runnin' fool!" We shot past somethin' that was just a black blur for a minute and then disappeared back in the dust. "What was that?" I yells.

"Montana!" screams Gloomy Gus, "and—"

"Ha! Ha!" roars the Kid, openin' his mouth for the first time. "That's goin' a few! Let me know when we pass Oregon, I got a friend there!"

"Montana Bill!" explains Gloomy Gus, frownin' at the Kid. "That's the only place you can get licker within five miles of Film City!" He looks at the Kid again and mutters half to himself, "Champion, eh!"

Then he yanks in the reins and we slow down to about a runaway's pace right near what looks to be a World's Fair with a big wall around it and an iron gate in the middle. We shot up to the entrance and the horse calls it a day and stops, puffin' and blowin' like a fat piano-mover.

"Film City!" hollers Gloomy Gus. "Git out here and walk in. Mr. Genaro's office is right back of the African Desert!"

I thanked him for bringin' us in alive. He didn't say nothin' to me, but as he was passin' in the gates I seen him lookin' after the Kid and shakin' his head. "Champion, hey!" he mumbles.

This Film City place would have made delerium tremens lay down and quit. There was Indians, cowboys, cannibals, chorus girls, Japs, sheriffs, train robbers, and—well, it looked like the place where they assemble dime novels. A guy goes racin' past us on a horse with a lot of maniacs, yellin' and shootin', tearin' after him and on the other side a gang of laborers in tin hats and short skirts is havin' a battle royal with swords. Three feet from where we're standin' a house is burnin' down and two guys is sluggin' each other on the roof. We walk along a little further and run into a private conversation. Some guy in a new dress suit is makin' love to a dame, while another fellow stands in front of them and says at the top of his voice, "Remember now, you're madly in love with her, but father detests the sight of your face. Ready—hey, camera—all right—wait a minute, wait a minute, don't wrestle with her, embrace her, will you, *em*brace her!"

Kid Scanlan takes this all in with his eyes poppin' out of his head and his mouth as open as a stuss game.

"Some joint, eh?" he says to me. "This is what I call a *regular* cabaret! See if we can get a table near the front!"

A lot of swell-lookin' dames comes in—well, of course it *was* some warm out there, but even at that they was takin' an awful chance on gettin' pneumonia, and files out of a house on the left and starts to dance and I had to drag the Kid away bodily. We duck through a side street, and every time we turn around some guy with a camera yells for us to get out of the way, but finally we wind up at Mr. Genaro's office. He ain't in, but a guy that was tells us Genaro's makin' a picture of Richard the Third, over behind the Street Scene in Tokio. We breezed over there and we found him.

Genaro is in the middle of what looks like the chorus of a burlesque show, only the men is wearin' tights instead of the women. I picked him out right away because he was the first guy I had seen in the place in citizen's clothes, outside of the guys with the kodaks. He was little and fat, lookin' more like a human plum puddin' than anything else. When we had worked our way through the mob, we saw that he was shakin' his fist at 'em and bawlin' 'em out.

"Are you Mr. Genaro?" I asks him.

"Joosta wait, joosta wait!" he hollers over his shoulder without even lookin' around. "I'm a ver' busy joosta now! Writa me the letta!"

"Where d'ye get that stuff?" I yells back, gettin' sore. "D'ye know who we are?"

I seen the rest of them gigglin', and Genaro dances around and throws up his hands.

"Aha!" he screams, pullin' at his hair. "You maka me crazy! What's a mat—what you want? Queek, don't make me wait!"

The Kid growls at him and whispers in my ear,

"Will I bounce him?"

"Not yet!" I tells him. "I'm Mr. Green," I says to Genaro, "and this is Kid Scanlan, welterweight champion of the world, and if you pull any more of that joosta wait stuff, you'll be able to say you fought him!"

He drops his hands and smiles.

"Excuse, please!" he says. "I maka mistake!" he grabs hold of his head again and groans, "Gotta bunch bonehead here this morning," he goes on, noddin' to 'em. "Driva me crazy! Shakespeare he see these feller play Reechard, he joomp out of he'sa grave!" He swings around at them all of a sudden and makes a face at 'em, "Broadaway star, eh?" he snarls. "Bah! You maka me seek! Go away for one, two hour. I senda for you—you all what you calla the bunk!"

On the level I thought he was gonna bite 'em!

The merry villagers scatter, and Genaro turns around to us and wipes his face with a red silk handkerchief.

"You knowa the piece?" he asks us. "Reechard the Third, Shakespeare?"

"Not quite!" I says. "What is he—a local scrapper?"

The Kid butts in and shoves me away.

"Don't mind this guy," he says to Genaro. "He's nothin' but a igrant roughneck! *I* got you right away. I remember in this Richard the Third thing—they's a big battle in the last act and Dick tells a gunman by the name of MacDuff to lay off him or he'll knock him for a goal!"

"Not lay off!" says Genaro, smiling "Lay on! Lay on, MacDuff!"

"Yeh?" inquires the Kid. "I thought it was lay off. I only seen the frolic once. I took off a member of Dick's gang at the Grand Oprey house, when I was broke in Trenton."

"Nex' week we start *your* picture," says Genaro to the Kid. "Mr. Van Aylstyne he'sa write scenario now. This gonna be great for you—magnificent! He'sa give you everything! Firsta reel you fall off a cliff!"

"Who, me?" hollers the Kid,

"Si!" smiles Genaro. "Bada man wanna feex you, so you no fighta the champ! You getta the beeg idea?"

"What's next?" asks the Kid, frownin'.

"Ah!" pipes Genaro, rollin' his eyes at the sky. "We giva you the whole picture! Second reel you get run over by train— fasta mail! You see? So you no fighta the champ!"

The Kid looks at me and grabs my arm.

"This guy's a maniac!" he hollers. "Did you get that railroad thing? He—"

Genaro goes right on like he don't hear him.

"Thirda reel!" he says. "Thirda reel you get hit by two automobiles, this bada feller try to feex you so you no fighta the champ!"

"Wait!" I butts in. "You must—"

"But fiftha reel—aaah!" Genaro don't pay no attention to me, but kisses his hand at a tree. "Fiftha reel," he says, "she'sa great! Get everybody excite! You get throw from sheep in ocean, fella shoot at you when you try sweem, bada fella come along in motorboat, he'sa run you down! Then you swim five, six, seven mile to land and there dozen feller beat you with club—so you no fighta the champ!"

The Kid has sunk down on a chair and he's fannin' himself. His face was the color of skim milk.

"What you think?" asks Genaro. "She's a maka fine picture, what?"

"Great!" I says. "If that guy that wants to fix the Kid so he no fighta the champ loses out, they can't say he wasn't tryin' anyhow! Why don't you throw in another reel, showin' the lions devourin' the Kid—so he no fighta the champ?"

"That's a good!" Genaro shakes his head. "I spika to Van Aylstyne!"

He took us up to his office and when we get inside the door they's a dame sittin' there which would make Venus look like a small-town soubrette. She looked like these other movie queens would like to! Whilst we're givin' her the up and down, she smiles at the Kid and he immediately drops his hat on the floor and knocks over a inkwell.

"Miss Vincent," says Genaro, "this Mr. Kid Scanlan. He'sa work with you nex' week. This Mr. Green, hisa fr'en'."

We shake hands all around and the Kid elbows me to one side.

"Where are you goin' this afternoon?" he asks the dame. "Anywheres?"

Genaro raps on the desk.

"Joosta one minoote!" he calls out. "Mr. Kid Scanlan, I would like—"

"Joosta wait!" pipes the Kid. "Writa me the letta! I'm ver' busy joosta now!" He puts one hand on the mantelpiece and drapes himself in front of the dame. "And you haven't been here long, eh?" he says.

Genaro frowns for a minute and then he grins and winks at me.

"Miss Vincent!" he butts in. "You show Mr. Kid Scanlan all around this afternoon, what? Explain him everything about nex' week we maka his picture. What you think, no?"

"Yes!" pipes the Kid grabbin' his hat. "I never been nowheres. Lets go!"

The dame smiles some more, and, well, Scanlan must have been born with a horseshoe in each hand because she takes his arm and they blow.

Just as they were goin' out the door, in comes Gloomy Gus which brought us up from the station. He looks at the Kid and this dame goin' out and he sneers after 'em.

"Champion!" he mutters, curlin' his lip. "Huh!"

The next mornin' we meet this guy Van Aylstyne who doped out the stuff so the Kid "no fighta the champ!" He's a tall, slim, gentle-lookin' bird, all dressed in white like a Queen of the May or somethin' and after hearin' him talk I figured my first guess was about right. We also got to know Edmund De Vronde, one of the leadin' men and the shop girls' delight, and him and Van Aylstyne were both members of the same lodge. Whilst we're standin' there talkin' to Genaro, who I found out was the headkeeper or somethin', along comes Miss Vincent in one of them trick autos that has a seat for two thin people and a gasoline tank. Only, you don't sit in 'em, you just stoop, with your knees jammed up against your chin. She drives this thing right up and stops where we're standin'. If she ever looked any better, she'd have fell for herself!

"I'm going to Long Beach," she sings out, "and I'm going to hit nothing but the tops of the trees! Come along?"

De Vronde, Van Aylstyne and the Kid left their marks at the same time, but you know, my boy was welterweight champ and when that auto buzzed away from there he went with it.

"Ugh!" remarks De Vronde. "I loathe those creatures!" He dusts off his sleeve where the Kid had grabbed it to toss him to one side. "The fellow struck me!" he says indignantly.

Van Aylstyne picks up his hat which had fell off in the struggle.

"Thank Heavens," he tells the other guy, "we will soon be rid of him! I'll have the script ready for Genaro to-morrow! I never saw such a vicious assault!"

They walked away, and I turns to Genaro who had stepped aside for a minute.

"Say!" I asks him. "Is this De Vronde guy worth anything to you?"

"*Sapristi*!" he tells me, makin' a face. "I could keel him! He'sa wan greata big what you call bunk! He'sa no good! He can't act, he can do nothing. Joosta got nice face—that's all!"

"Well," I says, "he won't have no nice face, if he don't lay off the Kid! If Scanlan hears him make any cracks about him like he just did now—well, he'll practically ruin him, that's all!"

After a while the Kid and Miss Vincent comes back and she hurries away to change her clothes because she's got to work in this Richard the Third thing. The Kid is all covered with dirt and mud and his face is all cut up from the flyin' pebbles and sand.

"Say!" he says to me. "That's some dame, believe me! We passed everything on the road from here to Long Beach and on the way back we beat the Sante Fe in by a city block! Come on over and see her work; she's gonna act in that Richard the Third thing!"

We breezed over past the African Desert and there's the troupe all gathered around a guy in his shirt sleeves, who's readin' 'em somethin' out of a book. One of the camera guys tells me it's Mr. Duke, Genaro's assistant.

"A fine piece of Camembert he is, too!" says this guy. "He put me over on this side to get the battle scene from an angle and tells me to shoot the minute the mêlée starts in case I don't get his signal. One of them dames fainted from the heat a minute ago and the rest of 'em go rushin' around yellin' like a lot of nuts. Naturally I thought the thing went in the picture and I took forty feet of it before he called me off! He's gonna report me now and I'm liable to get the gate when Genaro shows up! I'll *get* the big stew, though,—watch me!"

At this stage of the game, this Mr. Duke waves for us to come over.

"Where's Mr. Genaro?" he wants to know.

"Search me!" I tells him. "I just left him an hour or so ago and—"

He hurls down the book and dances around like he's gonna throw a fit or somethin'.

"I been all over the place," he yells, "and I can't find him! I want to get this exterior while the sun is right and there's no Richard or no Genaro!"

The Kid, who has been talkin' to Miss Vincent, comes over then and says,

"What's all the excitement?"

"Who are you?" asks Duke.

"We're from New York," I butts in, "and—"

"Well, sufferin' cats!" hollers Duke. "Why didn't you say so before? One of you is the man I'm holdin' this picture for!"

"Why, Genaro says," I begins, "that next week is—"

"Never mind Genaro!" shrieks Duke. "He ain't here now and I'm directing this picture! See that sun commencing to get dim? Which one of you was sent on by Mr. Potts?"

"This guy here!" I tells him, pointin' to the Kid. "I'm his manager."

"Carries a manager, does he?" snorts Duke. "Well, run

him in the dressin' room there and get a costume on him. Hurry up, will you—look at that sun!"

We beat it on the run for the place he pointed out, and as we started away I seen him throw out his chest and say to one of the dames,

"*That's* the way those stars should be handled all the time! Fussing over them is a mistake; you must show them at once that no such thing as temperament will be tolerated! Broadway star, eh? Well, you saw how *I* handled him!"

I didn't quite make that stuff, but I felt that somethin' was wrong somewheres. Genaro had told me the Kid's picture wasn't to be made for a week, but we were gettin' thirty thousand for this stunt so I says to the Kid,

"Get in there and shed them clothes of yours and I'll beat it over to the hotel and get your ring togs! They're gettin' ready to fix you so you no fighta the champ!"

I beat it back to the trick hotel and got the suitcase with the Kid's gloves, shoes and trunks in it and it didn't take me five minutes to get back, but that Duke guy is on my neck the minute he sees me.

"Will you hurry up?" he hollers, pullin' a watch on me. "Look at that sun!"

"He'll be out in a minute now!" I says. "I got a guy in there helpin' him dress."

"He knows this stuff all right, doesn't he?" he asks me. "I understand he's been doing nothing but the one line for years."

"Knows it?" I laughs. "He's the world's champion; that's good enough, ain't it?"

"That's what they all say!" he sneers. "All I hope is that he ain't no cheap ham! Look at that sun gettin' away from me!"

While I'm tryin' to dope out what all these birds in tights and with feathers in their hats has got to do with "How Kid Scanlan Won the Title," Duke grabs my arm.

"Drag that fellow out of the dressin' room," he says, "and

tell him he enters from the second entrance where those trees are. He goes right through the Tower scene—he knows it by heart, I guess. I'll be right up on that platform there directing and that's where he wants to face—not the camera!"

Well, I went into the dressin' room and the Kid is ready. He's got on a pair of eight ounce gloves, red silk trunks and ring shoes.

"What do I pull now?" he asks me.

"Just walk right out from between them trees," I says, "and they'll tip you off to the rest."

We sneaked around the scene from the back and stood behind the tree which Duke had pointed out. A stage hand or somethin' who seemed to be sufferin' from hysterics told us not to let Duke see us till we entered the scene, because it was considered bad luck to walk before the camera first.

"Clear!" we hear Duke yellin', and then he blows a whistle. "Hey, move faster there, you extra people, a little ginger! Billy, face center, can't you! Now, Miss Vincent, register fear— that's it, great! All right, Richard!"

"That's you!" pipes the stage hand, and on walks the Kid. He stands in the middle of the scene like he done many a time in the newspaper offices back home and strikes a fightin' pose.

A couple of women shrieks and runs back of the trees hidin' their faces and Miss Vincent falls in a chair and laughs herself sick. To say the Kid created a sensation would be puttin' it mild—he was a riot! The rest of the bunch howls out loud, holdin' their sides and staggerin' up against each other, and the stage hands rolled around the floor. But the guy that was runnin' the thing, this Duke person, almost faints, and then he gets red in the face and jumps down off the platform.

"What do you mean?" he screams at the Kid. "What do you mean by coming out before these ladies and gentlemen in that garb? How dare you? Is that your interpretation of Richard the Third? Have you been drinking or what?"

"What's the matter, pal?" asks the Kid, lookin' surprised. "I got to wear *somethin'*, don't I?"

Off goes the bunch howlin' again.

"If this is a joke, sir," yells Duke, "it will be a mighty costly one for you!"

This De Vronde has been standin' on the side lookin' on and the Kid, seein' Miss Vincent, waves a glove at her. She waves back holdin' her side and smiles.

"Haw! Haw! Haw!" roars this De Vronde guy. "How droll!"

The Kid is over to him in two steps. He's seen that everybody is givin' him the laugh and he realizes he's in wrong somehow, but the thing has him puzzled.

"Where d'ye get that 'haw, haw' stuff?" he snarls, stickin' his chin out in front of De Vronde.

"Why, you ignorant ass!" sneers De Vronde, out loud, so's Miss Vincent can hear him. "If you had any brains you'd know!"

"I don't need no brains!" snaps the Kid, settin' himself. "I got *this*!"

And he drops De Vronde with a right hook to the jaw!

"Boys!" screams Duke, pointin' to the Kid. "Throw that ruffian out!"

A couple of big huskies makes a dash for the Kid, and I figured I might as well get in the thing now as later, so I tripped one as he was goin' past and the Kid bounces the other with a short left. De Vronde jumps up and hits the Kid over the head with a cane, while Miss Vincent screams and hollers "Coward!" Then a bunch of supers comes runnin' in from the back just as the Kid puts De Vronde down for keeps, and in a minute everybody was in there tryin'.

Everybody but one guy, and he was turnin' the crank of his camera like he was gettin' paid by the number of revolutions the thing made.

While it lasted, it was some fracas, as we say at the studio. It certainly was a scream to see them guys, all dressed up to play the life out of Richard the Third, fallin' all over each other to get out of the way of the Kid's arms and bein' held back by the jam behind 'em. After the Kid has beat most of them up and I have took care of a few myself, a whistle blows and they all fall back— and in rushes Genaro.

"Sapristi!" he hollers. "What you mean eh? What you people do with my Reechard?"

Duke tries to see him out of his one good eye.

"This scoundrel," he pipes, pointin' to the Kid, "came out here to play Richard the Third costumed like that!"

Genaro looks from me to the Kid and grabs his head.

"What?" he yells. "That feller want to play Reechard? Ho, ho! You maka me laugh! You're crazy lika the heat! That's what you call fighting champion of the world! He'sa Mr. Kid Scanlan. We maka hisa picture nex' week!"

Duke gives a yell and falls in a chair.

I pulls on my coat and wipes my face with a handkerchief.

"Yes," I says, "and they just tried to fix him so he no fighta the champ!"

"Zowie!" pipes Duke, sprawled out in the chair, "I thought he was Roberts, the man we wired to come on from Boston! What in the name of Charlie Chaplin will we do now? Potts will be here to-morrow to see this picture and you know what it means, if it isn't made!"

The Kid is over talkin' to Miss Vincent and Genaro calls him over.

"*Viola*!" he tells him. "You see what you do? You spoil the greata picture, the actor, the everything! To-morrow Mr. Potts he'sa come here. 'Where's a Reechard the Third, Genaro?' he'sa wanna know. I tella him—then, good-by everybody!"

"Everything would have been O.K.," says the Kid, pointin' to De Vronde who's got a couple of dames workin' over him with smellin' salts. "Everything would have been O.K. at that, if Stupid over there hadn't gimme the haw, haw!"

We go back to the dressing-room and the Kid gets on his clothes. That night, findin' that we was as welcome in Film City as smallpox, we went over to Frisco and saw the town.

When we come back the next mornin' and breeze in the gates, the first thing we see is Gloomy Gus that drove us up from the station.

"Say!" he sings out. "You fellers are gonna get it good! The boss is here."

"Yeh?" says the Kid. "Where's Miss Vincent?"

"Talkin' to the boss!" he answers. "I don't believe you're no fighter, either!"

"Where was you yesterday?" I asks him.

"Mind yer own business!" he snaps. He gives the Kid the up and down. "Champion of the world!" he sneers. "Huh!"

"Go 'way!" the Kid warns him. "I got enough work yesterday!"

"I think you're a big bluff!" persists the gloomy guy, puttin' up his hands and circlin' around the Kid. "Come on and fight or acknowledge yore master!"

He makes a pass at the Kid and the Kid steps inside of it and drops him, just as a big auto comes roarin' past and stops. Out hops friend Potts, the guy that practically give us our start in the movies. In other words, the thirty thousand dollar kid!

"Well, well!" he pipes, lookin' at the gloomy guy on the turf and then at us. "What does this mean, sir? Are you trying to annihilate all my employees? Do you know you cost me a small fortune yesterday by ruining that Richard the Third picture?"

"I'm sorry, boss," the Kid tells him, proddin' Gloomy Gus carelessly with his foot, "but all your hired men jumped at me at once and a guy has to protect himself, don't he?"

"Nonsense!" grunts Potts. "You assaulted Mr. De Vronde and temporarily disabled several of my best people! I had made all arrangements for the release of that Shakespeare picture in two days, and you have put me in a terrible hole!"

"Now, listen," I butts in, "I tried to—"

"Not a word!" he cuts me off, wavin' his hands. "One of the camera men, another infernal idiot, kept turning the crank while this disgraceful brawl was at its height and I have proof of your villainy on film! I'll use it as a basis to sever my contract with you and—"

"Slow up!" I says. "If you lay down on the thirty thousand iron men, I'll pull a suit on you!"

Along comes a guy and touches Potts on the arm.

"They're waiting for you in the projecting room," he says.

"Come with me—both of you!" barks Potts, "and see for yourself the damage you caused!"

We followed him around to a little dark room with three or four chairs in it and a sheet on one wall. De Vronde, Miss Vincent, Duke and Genaro are there waitin' for us.

Well, they start to show the picture, and everything is all right up to the time the Kid busted into the drama. Now I hadn't seen nothin' out of the way at the time it actually happened, but here in this little room it was a riot when they showed it on the sheet. You could see Scanlan wallop De Vronde and then in another second the massacre is on full blast!

On the level, it was the funniest thing I'd seen in a long time. A guy with lockjaw would have to laugh at it. Here was the Kid knockin' 'em cold as fast as they come on, with their little trick hats and the pink silk tights. There was a pile of Shakespeare actors a foot deep all around him as far as you could see. Potts is laughin' louder than anybody in the place, and when they finally shut the thing off he slaps the Kid on the back.

"Great!" he hollers. "Wonderful! Who directed that?"

"*I* did!" pipes Duke, throwin' out his chest. "Some picture, eh?"

"Joosta one minoote!" says Genaro, wakin' up, "joosta one minoote! It was under my supervision, Mr. Potts! I feexa the —"

"Cut that strip of film off!" Potts interrupts, "and take four more reels based on the same idea! Get somebody to write a scenario around a fighter busting into the drama and playing Shakespeare! It's never been done, and if the rest of it is as funny as that it will be a knockout!"

"But Reechard!" says Genaro. "What of heem?"

"Drop it!" snaps Potts. "Everybody get to work on this and I'll stay here till it's finished!"

I looked around and pipe the Kid—over talkin' to Miss Vincent, of course.

"Say!" he wants to know. "Do we go to Oakland in that rabbit-chaser of yours this afternoon, Miss Vincent?"

"Sir!" butts in De Vronde. "This lady and I are conversing!"

"Now listen, Cutey!" smiles the Kid. "You know what happened yesterday, don't you?"

De Vronde turns pale and Miss Vincent giggles.

"Of course we're going to Oakland!" she laughs. "I'm going to be your leading woman next week in 'How Kid Scanlan Won the Title.'"

"Suits me!" says the Kid. "But say, on the level now—I'm there forty-seven ways on that Shakespeare thing, ain't I?"

CHAPTER II
EAST LYNCH

Success has ruined more guys than failure ever will. It's like a Santa Cruz rum milk punch on an empty stomach—there's very few people can stand it. Many a guy that's a regular fellow at a hundred a month, becomes a boob at a hundred a week. What beat Napoleon, Caesar and Nero—failure? No, success! Give the thing the once over some time and you'll see that I'm right.

Success is the large evenin' with the boys at the lodge and failure is the mornin' after. As a matter of fact, they're twins. Often you can be a success without knowin' it, so if you been a failure all your life accordin' to your own dope, cheer up. But when you get up to the top where you can look down at all these other guys tryin' to sidestep the banana peels of life and climb up with you, knock off thinkin' what a big guy you are for a minute and give ten minutes to thinkin' what a tough time you had gettin' there. Give five minutes more to ruminatin' on how long the mob remembers a loser and you'll find it the best sixteen minutes you ever spent in your life.

In these days when the world is just a great big baby yellin' for a new toy every second, any simp can beat his way to the top. The real stunt is *stayin' there* after you arrive!

Kid Scanlan was a good sample of that. When the Kid was fightin' for bean money and the exercise, he never spent nothin' but the evenin' and very little of that. He didn't know whether booze was a drink or a liniment and the only ladies he was bothered about was his mother. But when he knocked out One-Punch Ross for the title and eased himself into the movies, it was all different. He begin to spend money like a vice-investigating committee, knock around with bartenders and give in to all the strange desires that hits a guy with his health and a bankroll. I stood by and cheered for a while until he crashes in love with this movie queen, Miss Vincent, that got more money a start than

26

the Kid did in a season and more letters from well wishin' males than a newly elected mayor. Then I stepped in and saved the Kid just before he become a total loss.

I was standin' by the African Desert one day watchin' them take a picture called "Rapacious Rupert's Revenge," when the Kid comes over and calls me aside. Since he had become a actor he had gave himself up to dressin' in panama hats, Palm Beach suits and white shoes. He reminded me of the handsome young lieutenant in a musical comedy. Every time I seen him in that outfit I expected to hear him burst into some song like, "All hail, the Queen comes thither!" Know what I mean?

Well, havin' lured me away under the shade of some palm trees, the Kid tells me he's goin' over to Frisco on a little shoppin' expedition, and he wants me to come with him. I says I can't drink a thing because I have had a terrible headache since the night before when him and me and some camera men went to Montana Bill's and toyed with the illegal brew for a few hours.

"That last round," I says, "which I'll always remember because it come to six eighty-five, was what ruined me. The bartender must have gone crazy and put booze in them cocktails, because I've had that headache ever since!"

"It ain't the cocktails that give you the headache," the Kid tells me, "it was the check. And you must have had a bun on before that, anyhow, because you paid it! But that's got nothin' to do with this here trip to Frisco. I'm not goin' to stop anywheres for no powders. I'm gonna get somethin' I've needed for a long time!"

"What is it," I asks him, "a clean collar?"

"I wish you'd save that comedy for some rainy Sunday," he says; "that stuff of yours is about as funny as a broken arm! Since I been out here with these swell actors, I been changin' my clothes so often that I'll bet my body thinks I'm kiddin' it. Stop knockin' and come over to Frisco with me and—"

I don't know what else he was goin' to say, because just at

that minute a Kansas cyclone on wheels come between us and I come to in a ditch about five feet from where the Kid is tryin' to see can he really stand on his head. When I had picked up enough ambition to get to my feet, I went over and jacked up the Kid. About half a mile up the road the thing which had attacked us is turnin' around.

"Run for your life!" I yells to the Kid. "It's comin' back!"

Before we could pick our hidin' places, the thing has drawed up in front of us and we see it's one of them trick autos known to the trade as racin' cars. I recognized it right away as belongin' to Miss Vincent. The owner was in the car and beside her was Edmund De Vronde, the shop-girls' delight. The Kid and De Vronde had took to each other from the minute they first met like a ferret does to a rat. It was a case of hate at first sight. So you can figure that this little incident did nothin' to cement the friendship. Miss Vincent leaps out of the thing and comes runnin' over to us.

"Good Heavens!" she says. "You're not hurt, are you?"

She's lookin' right past me and at the Kid like it made little or no difference whether *I* was damaged or not.

The Kid throws half an acre of California out of his collar and removes a few pebbles and a cigar butt from his ear.

"No!" he growls, with a sarcastical smile. "Was they many killed?"

She takes out a little trick silk handkerchief and wipes off his face with it.

"I meant to step on the foot brake," she explains, "and I must have stepped on the gas by mistake!"

"You must have stepped on the dynamite," I butts in, "because it blowed me into the ditch!"

The Kid shakes a bucket or so of sand out of his hair and looks over at the car where De Vronde is examin' us through a pair of cheaters and enjoyin' himself scandalously.

"I see you got Foolish with you," says the Kid to Miss

Vincent. "What's the matter—are you off me now?"

She smiles and wipes some mud off the Kid's collar.

"Why, no," she tells him. "Genaro is putting on 'The Escapes of Eva' this morning and I'm playing the lead opposite Mr. De Vronde. I happened to pick him up on the road and I'm bringing him in, that's all."

"Yeh?" says the Kid, still lookin' over at the car. "What are *you* laughin' at, Stupid?" he snarls suddenly at De Vronde.

De Vronde give a shiver and the glasses fell off in the bottom of the car. While he was stoopin' down to look for 'em, the Kid turns to Miss Vincent.

"I only wish he had been drivin' the thing," he says, "because then I'd have some excuse for bouncin' him! On the level, now," he goes on, winkin' at her, "he *was* drivin' the thing, wasn't he?"

"Oh, no!" she answers. "I was at the wheel."

The Kid frowns and thinks for a minute.

"Well," he says finally, takin' another look at De Vronde, "ain't the brakes or somethin' where he was sittin'?"

"No!" she tells him, grabbin' him by the arm. "Please don't lose your head now and start a fuss! I'm awfully sorry this happened, but as long as neither of you were hurt and—"

"It didn't do me no *good*, that's a cinch!" butts in the Kid, with a meanin' look at his spoiled scenery. He walks over to the car and glares up at De Vronde. "Hey!" he snarls. "What d'ye mean by bein' in a automobile that runs over me, eh?"

De Vronde moves as far over as the seat will let him, and then falls back on prayer.

"I must decline to enter any controversy with you," he pipes, after a minute. "You were standing in the right of way and —"

The Kid grins and holds up his hand. His face has lighted all up and he's lickin' his lips like he always did in the ring when he seen the other guy was pickin' out a place to fall. He's walked around to where De Vronde had been sittin' and piped a little handle stickin' up.

"What's this?" he calls to Miss Vincent, who's climbin' in the other side.

"That's just the oil pump," she says.

The Kid suddenly reaches up, grabs De Vronde by the arm and jerks him out of the car.

"You big stiff!" he roars. "Why didn't you pump that oil, hey? If you had done that, the thing wouldn't have hit us! I knowed it was all your fault—you deliberately laid off that pump, hopin' we'd get killed!"

With that he starts an uppercut from the ground, but I yanked him away just as De Vronde murmurs, "Safety first!" and takes a dive. Miss Vincent gets out and gives me a hand with the Kid, and De Vronde sits up and menaces us with his cane.

"That isn't a bit nice!" Miss Vincent frowns at the Kid. "That's ruffianly! You never should have struck him!"

"I didn't hit him!" yells the Kid. "The big tramp quit! If I had hit him he wouldn't be gettin' up."

He starts over again, but I held him until she has climbed into the car with De Vronde and they shoot up the road. Just before they disappeared, De Vronde turns around in the seat and shakes his finger at us.

"Only the presence of the lady," he calls, "saves you from my wrath!"

"Come on!" says the Kid, grabbin' my arm. "Let's get the next train for Frisco, before I run after that guy and flatten him! Believe me," he goes on, lookin' up the road after the car, "I'll get that bird before the day is over if I have to bust a leg!"

And that's just what he did—both!

All the way over in the train I tried to work the third degree on the Kid to find out what he was goin' to buy, but there was nothin' doin'. He stalled me off until we pull into the town and then he takes me to a street that was so far from the railroad station I come near castin' a shoe on the way over. About half way down this boulevard there's a garage and the Kid stops in front of it.

"Wait here!" he tells me. "And don't let nobody give you no babies to mind. I'll be right out!"

He slips inside and I'm lookin' the joint over when a big sign catches my eye. I took one good flash at the thing, and then I starts right in after the Kid. A friend of mine in New York had gone into a place with a sign on it like that one time and made a purchase. Six months later when he come out of the hospital, he claimed the bare smell of gasoline made him faint Here's what it said on that sign,

J. MARKOWITZ
USED AND NEARLY NEW AUTOS
FOR SALE

It was kinda dark inside and it takes me a minute to get my bearin's, but finally I see the Kid and a snappy dressed guy standin' in front of what I at first thought was a Pullman sleeper. When I get a close up, though, I find it's only a tourin' car. It was the biggest automobile I ever seen in my life; a sightseein' bus would have looked like a runabout alongside of it. There was one there and it did! The thing hadn't been painted since the *Maine* was blowed up, and you could see the guy that had been keepin' it was fond of the open air, because there was samples of mud from probably all over the world on it.

"You could believe it, you're gettin' it a practically brand new car!" the young feller is tellin' the Kid. "The shoes are in A number one condition—all they need is now vulcanizin', and Oi! —how that car could travel!"

"Just a minute!" I butts in. "Before you make this sale, I want to speak to my friend here."

Both him and the Kid glares at me, and the Kid pushes me

aside.

"Lay off!" he says. "I know just what you're gonna say. There's no use of you tryin' to discourage me, because I'm gonna buy a car. Here I am makin' all kinds of money and I might as well be a bum!—no automobile or nothin'. I should have had a car long ago; all the big leaguers own their own tourin' cars. There's no class to you any more, if you don't flit from place to place in your own bus!"

"Yeh?" I comes back. "Well, Washington never had no car, but that didn't stop *him* from gettin' over! I never heard of Columbus gettin' pinched for speedin' and Shakespeare never had no trouble with blowouts. Yet all them birds was looked on as the loud crash in their time. What's the answer to that?"

In butts I. Markowitz, shovin' his hat back on his ears.

"That brings us right down to the present!" he says. "And I could tell you why none of your friends had oitermobiles. Cars was too expensive in them days—a millionaire even would have to talk it over with his wife before they should buy one. But now, almost they give them away! Materials is cheaper, in Europe the war is over and now competition is—is—more! That's why I'm able to let your friend have this factory pet here for eight hundred dollars. A bargain you ask me? A man never heard a bargain like that!"

"Don't worry!" I tells him. "Nobody will ever hear about it from me. If you made him a present of it and throwed in the garage, it would still be expensive!"

"Who's buyin' this car?" snarls the Kid. "You or me?"

"Not guilty!" I says. "If you got to have a car, why don't you buy a new one?"

"This is the same as new!" pipes I. Markowitz.

"Speak when you're spoken to, Stupid!" I says.

"Don't start nothin' here," the Kid tells me, pullin' me away. "I don't want none of them new cars. They're too stiff and I might go out and hit somebody the first crack out of the box. I want one that's been broke in."

"Well," I laughs, "that's what you're gettin', believe me! That there thing has been broke in and out!" I turns to I. Markowitz. "What make is the old boiler?" I asks him.

"Boiler he calls it!" he says, throwin' up his hands and lookin' at the ceilin'. "It's an A. G. F. I suppose even you know what an A number one car that is, don't you?"

"No!" I answers. "But I know what A. G. F. means."

He falls.

"What?" he wants to know.

"Always Gettin' Fixed!" I tells him. "They make all them used cars. I know a guy had two of them and between 'em they made a fortune for three garages and five lawyers! How old is it?"

"Old!" says I. Markowitz, recovering "Who said it was old? Your wife should be as young as that car! It was turned in here last week, only eight short days from the factory. The owner was sudden called he should go out of town and—"

"And he went somewheres and got an automobile to make the trip," I cuts him off, "and left this thing here!"

"Don't mind him!" says the Kid, gettin' impatient. "Gimme a receipt." He digs down for the roll.

While I. Markowitz is countin' the money with lovin' fingers, I went around to one side of the so called auto and looked at the speedometer. One flash at the little trick clock was ample.

"Stop!" I yells, glarin' at him. "How long did you say this car had been out of the factory?"

"Right away he hollers at me!" says I. Markowitz to the Kid. "A week."

"Well," I tells him, "all I got to say is that the bird that had it must have been fleein' the police! He certainly seen a lot of the world, but I can't figure how he slept. He was what you could call a motorin' fool. It says on this speedometer here,

45,687 miles and if that guy did it in a week, I got to hand it to him! I'll bet he's so nutty over speed that he's goin' around now bein' shot out of cannons from place to place, eh?"

I. Markowitz gets kinda balled up and blows his nose twice.

"That must be the—the—motor number!" he stammers.

"Sure!" nods the Kid. "Don't mind him, he's always got the hammer out. Count that change and gimme a receipt."

"Wait!" I says. "Gimme one more chance to save you from givin' yourself the work. Have you heard the motor turn over? Does the clutch slip in all right? Do the brakes work? Has the—"

"Say!" butts in the Kid. "What d'ye think I been doin'—workin' here at nights? Don't mind him," he tells I. Markowitz, who ain't. "Hurry up with that receipt!"

"How is the motor?" I asks that brigand. "Tell me that, will you?"

"Convalescent!" he sneers, tuckin' the Kid's bankroll away.

"Some motor, eh?" pipes the Kid. "And it's got a one-man top on it besides, ain't it?" he asks I. Markowitz.

"Why not?" says he. "Everything new and up to date you would find on this car which only yesterday I could have sold to a feller for a thousand dollars!"

After pullin' that, he walks over to the thing and climbs in the back. "An example!" he says. "If you're alone in the car and there's nobody with you, you only should stand up on the seat and pull up the top like this, if it comes up a rain. Then you—"

I didn't hear the rest on account of him havin' trouble makin' his voice travel from under the seat, because he reached up and pulled somethin' here and jerked somethin' there—and that one-man top made good! I thought at first the ceilin' of the joint had fell in, and I'll bet I. Markowitz *knowed* it had, but then I seen it was only the thing that keeps the rain out of the car.

Me and the Kid drags him out, and as soon as he gets on his feet and felt to see if he had his watch and so forth, he wipes the dirt out of his eyes and turns on me.

"It's a wonder I ain't now dead on account from you?" he snarls. "I suppose you're one of them wise fellers from New Jersey, which they got to be showed everything, heh?"

"Missouri!" I says. "Not New Jersey. If I was from New Jersey, I would probably be fightin' with the Kid to let *me* buy the car!"

"It's got a self-commencer on it, too!" yelps the Kid, climbin' into the front seat. "See—lookit!" He presses a button with his foot and a laughin' hyena or somethin' in the hood moans a couple of times and then passes away.

"The first time I wouldn't be surprised you should have to crank it," says I. Markowitz. "The motor has been standin' so long—I mean—that is—speakin' of motors, I think that one is maybe a little cold! Once she gets runnin' everything will be A number one!"

I goes around the front of the thing and stoops down.

"Put her on battery, if there's any on there," I calls to the Kid, "and I'll spin the motor!"

I. Markowitz steps over and lays his hand on my arm. His face is as serious as prohibition.

"Its only fair I should tell you," he whispers, "that she kicks a little!"

I give him a ungrateful look and grabs hold of the crank. After turnin' the thing ninety-four times without gettin' nothin' but a blister on my thumb, I quit.

"Nothin' stirrin'," I remarks to I. Markowitz.

"Believe me, that's funny!" he tells me, shakin' his head like he had ball bearin's in his neck.

"Ain't it?" I says. "Are you positive they's a motor inside there?"

He makes a funny little noise in his throat and not

knowin' him long, I didn't know what he meant. There's a big husky in overalls walkin' by with plenty of medium oil on his face and a monkey wrench in his hand. I. Markowitz hisses at him, and they exchange jokes in some foreign language for a minute and then the new-comer grabs hold of that crank like the idea was to see if he could upset the car in three twists. He gives it a turn, and I guess the Kid had got to monkeyin' around them little buttons on the steerin' wheel because it went off like a cannon. First, there was a great big bang! And then a cloud of smoke rolls out of the back of the car and the bird that had wound the thing up come to in an oil can, half way across the floor. The Kid fell off the seat and me and I. Markowitz busted the hundred yard record to the front door.

"That was a rotten trick, wasn't it?" I asks him when we stopped.

"What do you talk tricks?" he pants.

"Why," I tells him, "puttin' that dynamite in the hood!"

"That wasn't dynamite," he says. "She only backfired a little. I wouldn't be surprised if it turned out there was, now, too much air in the carburetor. The only reason I ran out here is because I seen it passin' a friend of mine and—"

"I know," I cuts him off. "I seen it too!"

We go back to the Kid and his play toy, and he's leanin' up against the side of it rubbin' his shoulder and scowlin'.

"What kind of stuff was that, eh?" he growls at I. Markowitz. "I liked to broke my neck!"

"'Snothin'!" says he, pattin' the Kid on the back and smilin'. "You could do that with a new car, you could take my word for it. It's all, now, experience!" He looks around. "Herschel!" he hollers.

It turns out that Herschel is the guy that had wound the thing up, and he gets out of the oil can and comes over, mutterin' to himself and glarin' at all of us. He takes off the hood and stalls around it with a hammer and a monkey wrench for a minute, still mutterin' away, and you could see he wasn't wishin' us no luck. Finally, he puts the hood on again and walks around to the crank.

"As soon as you could hear it buzz," he grunts at the Kid, "you should give her some gas."

I stood aside and picked out my exit, and I. Markowitz seen his friend passin' again so he started for the door. The Kid says we're both yellah and climbs gamely back into the seat. Herschel stops mutterin' long enough to give the crank a turn, which same he did. This time there was no shots fired, but the thing begins the darndest racket I ever heard in my life. A boiler factory would have quit cold alongside of that motor and a cavalry charge would have gone unnoticed on the same floor. I asked I. Markowitz what broke, and he says nothin' but that the noise is caused by the motor bein' so powerful, fifty horse power, he claimed.

"You can't tell me," I says, backin' away from the thing, "that no fifty horses could make that much noise, not even if they was crazy! The guy that brought that in here must have tied a lot of machine guns together with a fuse and Stupid there set 'em off when he turned the crank!"

He runs around to the side where the Kid is and shuts down the gas and I seen half of Frisco lookin' in the door, figurin' the Japs had got started at last, or else somebody was puttin' on a dress rehearsal of the Civil War.

"Ain't she a beauty?" screams I. Markowitz to the Kid, barely makin' himself heard over the din. "Give a listen how that motor turns over—not a break or a miss and as smooth like glass! That's hittin' on six, all right!"

"I'm glad to hear that," I says. "I'm glad it's only six, because the thing will have to quit pretty soon. There ain't no six nothin's could stand up under that hittin' much longer!"

I. Markowitz steps on the runnin' board and holds on with both hands. He had to, because that motor had got the car doin' a muscle dance.

"Where d'ye want to go?" he yells to the Kid. "I'll have Herschel take you out so he should show you everything."

"Tell him to wash his face instead!" the Kid hollers back. "I don't need nobody to show me nothin' about a car. Come on!" he yells at me. "All aboard for Film City!"

"Ha! Ha!" I sneers. "Rave on! I wouldn't get in that thing for Rockefeller's bankroll!"

I had to holler at the top of my voice to drown out that motor.

"C'mon!" yells the Kid. "Don't be so yellah—you got everybody lookin' at you. She's all right now, and as soon as she gets warmed up she'll be rollin' along in great shape!"

"Yes!" I says. "And so will I—in a day coach of the Sante Fe!"

Well, he coaxed, threatened and so-forthed me, until finally I took a chance and climbed in beside him. The populace at the doors give three cheers and wished us good luck as we banged and rattled through their midst. We went on down the street, attractin' no more attention than the German army would in London, and every time we turned a new corner people run out of their houses to see was there a parade comin'. We passed several sure enough automobiles and they sneered at us, and one of them little flivvers got so upset by the noise that it blowed out a tire as we went by. Finally, we come to the city line and the Kid says he figures it's about time to see can the thing travel. He monkeys around them strange buttons on the steerin' wheel, pulls a handle here and there and presses a lever with his foot. The minute he did that we got action! That disappearin' cannon in the back went off three times and I bet it blowed up all the buildin's in the block. There was a horse and buggy passin' at the time and the guy that was drivin' it don't know what happened yet, because at the first bang, that horse started for the old country and it must have been Lou Dillon—believe me, it could run! I looked back and watched it. A big cloud of smoke rolls up from the back of the car, and I seen guys runnin' out of stores and wavin' to us with their fists and then a couple of brave and bold motorcycle cops jumps on their fiery steeds and falls in behind.

I guess the ex-owner of this bus was on the level at that about doin' them forty-five thousand miles in a week, because this car could have beat a telegram across the country, "when she got warmed up!" as I. Markowitz says. Every one of them six cylinders was in there trying and when they worked together like little pals and forgot whatever private quarrels they had, the result was *speed*, believe me! The Kid was hangin' on to the steerin' wheel and havin' the time of his young life and I was hangin' on to the seat and wishin' I had listened to that insurance agent in New York. We come to the top of a hill and as we start down the other side the prize boob of the county is waterin' the pavement around his real estate. When he hears us, he drops the hose which makes it all wet in front of us.

"Hold tight!" screams the Kid to me. "We're gonna do a piece of skiddin'. I forgot to get chains!"

Just about then we hit the damp spot and the Kid puts on the brakes. Sweet Cookie! You should have seen that car! It must have got sore at the man with the hose and went crazy, because it made eight complete turns tryin' to get at him and the poor simp was too scared to run. Finally the thing gives it up and shoots down to the bottom of the hill. We hit a log and I hit the one-man top. Then the motor calls it a day and stops dead. The Kid hops out and walks around to the crank. He gives it a couple of turns and it turns right back at him. He grabs it again and it was short with a left hook to the jaw, and then the Kid shakes his head and takes off one side of the hood. He sticks his hand down inside and pulls out a little brown thing that looks like a cup with a cover on it.

"No wonder she stopped!" he says, holdin' it up. "Look

what I just found in here."

I give it the once over.

"What d'ye think of that, eh?" he says. "It's a wonder she run at all! I'll bet that boob mechanic left that in there when he started us off at the garage." He throws the thing in a ditch and puts the hood on. "Now," he says, "we're off for Film City!"

He grabs hold of the crank and gives it about eleven whirls, but there ain't a thing doin' and while we're stuck there like that, along comes a guy in another car.

"Can I help you fellows out?" he hollers.

"Yes!" I yells back. "Have you got a rope?"

He comes over and looks at the thing.

"What seems to be the trouble?" he asks the Kid.

"Nothin' in particular," the Kid tells him. "She's a great little car only we can't get her goin'."

"Have you got gas?" asks the stranger.

"Plenty!" says the Kid. "D'ye think I would try to run a car without gasoline?"

"I don't know," says the other guy. "I never seen you before! Is your spark all right?"

"A number one!" pipes the Kid.

"And she won't run?" he asks.

"She won't run!" we both says together.

"Hmph!" he snorts, scratchin' his head. He opens the hood and fusses around on both sides for a minute and then he rubs the side of his nose with his finger. He looks like he was up against a tough proposition.

"How far have you run this car?" he asks the Kid finally.

"All the way from Frisco," answers the Kid.

"Like this?" he says, pointin' to the motor.

"No!" I cuts in. "It was movin'."

"Why you couldn't have gone three feet with this car!" he busts out suddenly. "I never seen nothin' like this before in my life!"

"Why don't you go out at nights, then?" growls the Kid, gettin' sore. "Stop knockin' and tell us what's the matter with it."

"There ain't nothin' the matter with it," says the other guy with an odd little grin. "Not a thing—*only it ain't got no carburetor in it, that's all*!"

If he figured on creatin' a sensation on that remark—and from the way he said it, he did—he lost the bet. The Kid just gives him the baby stare and shrugs his shoulders like it's past him.

"No which?" he says.

"Carburetor!" explains the native. "The little cup where your gasoline mixes with the air to start the motor."

The Kid claps his hands together and yells,

"That little crook back in Frisco must have held out on me!"

But I had been doin' some thinkin' and I looks the Kid in the eye,

"What does this carburetor thing look like?" I asks the other guy.

He describes it to me, and when he got all through I gives the Kid another meanin' look and walks over to the ditch. After pawin' around in the mud for a while I found the little cup the Kid had throwed away.

"Is this it?" I asks the native.

"It is," he says. "What was it doin' over there?"

"It must have fell off!" answers the Kid quickly, kickin' at me to keep quiet.

Well, this guy finally fixes us up and about an hour later we hit the little road that leads into Film City, without havin' no further mishaps except the noise from that motor. About half a mile from the gates I seen a familiar lookin' guy standin' in the middle of the road and wavin' his hands at us.

"Slow up!" I says to the Kid. "Here's Genaro!"

The Kid reaches down to the side of his seat and yanks a

handle that was stickin' up. It come right off in his hand and we kept right on goin'.

"That's funny!" says the Kid, holdin' up the handle and lookin' at it like it's the first one he ever seen. "We should have stopped right away—that's the emergency brake!"

He stamps on the floor with his foot a couple of times and shuts off the gas. We drift right on, and, if Genaro had had rheumatism, he would have been killed outright. As it was, he jumped aside just in time and the car comes to a stop of its own free will about twenty feet past him down the road.

"What's a mat?" yells Genaro, rushin' up to us. "Why you no stoppa the car when you see me?"

"Why don't they stop prohibition?" I hollers back at him. "We must have lost the stopper off this one, we—"

But he runs around the other side to where the Kid is sitting examinin' all them handles and buttons.

"*Sapristi*!" he yells at the Kid. "Where you go, Meester Kid Scanlan? Everybody she's a look for you—Meester Potts he'sa want you right away! We starta firsta reel of your picture to-day. Everybody she'sa got to wait for you!"

"Keep your shirt on!" growls the Kid. "You told me this mornin' I had lots of time, didn't you?"

Genaro grabs hold of a tree and does a little dance.

"Aha!" he remarks to the sky. "He'sa make me crazee! What you care what I tole you this a morning? Joosta now I want you queek! You maka mucha talk with me while Meester Potts and everybody she'sa wait for you!"

"Well," says the Kid. "Get in here and we'll go there right away."

Genaro climbs in the back of the car.

"Hurry up!" he says, holdin' his ears. "Anything so she'a stop that terrible noise. Hurry up!"

"I'll do that little thing!" pipes the Kid—and we was off.

I climbed over the seat and in the back with Genaro so's

he wouldn't feel lonesome, and, so's if the Kid hit anything, I'd have a little more percentage in my favor. Genaro seems to be sore about something and to make conversation I ask him what's the matter.

"Everything she's the matter!" he tells me, while the Kid keeps his foot on the gas and we bump and clatter along the road. "Everything she's the matter! I work all morning on lasta reel of 'The Escapes of Eva.' Got two hundred extra people stand around do nothing. De Vronde, the bigga bunk, he's a play lead with Miss Vincent." He stops and kisses his hand at a tree we was passing "Ah!" he goes on. "She'sa fina girl! Some time maybe I ask her—pardone, I talka too fast! Lasta reel De Vronde he'sa get what you call lynched. They putta rope around he'sa neck and he's a stand under bigga tree. Joosta as they pulla rope to keel him, Miss Vincent," he throws another kiss at a tree. "Ah! sucha fina girl!" he whispers at me rollin' his eyes. "Sometime I —pardone, everytime I forget! Miss Vincent she'sa come along on horse and sava he'sa life—you see?"

"I got you!" I tells him. "Then what happens?"

"*Sapristi*!" he says. "That's all! What you want for five reels? But thisa morning, Meester Potts he'sa come up and watch. He'sa president of company and knows much about money, but acting—bah! he'sa know nothing! Gotta three year old boy he'sa know more! He'sa standa there and smile and rub he'sa hands together lika barber while we taka lasta reel. Everything she'sa fine till we come to place where De Vronde he'sa get lynch and Miss Vincent—ah!—she'sa come up on horse and sava him. Then Meester Potts he'sa rush over and stoppa the cameras. 'No!' he'sa yell. 'No, by Heaven, I won't stand for that! That's a rotten! You got to get difference ending froma that!'"

"What was the matter?" I asks him. "Didn't he want De Vronde saved?"

His shoulders does one of them muscle dances.

"Ask me!" he says. "I couldn't tella you! He'sa know

nothing about art! Joosta money—that's all. He'sa tella me girl saving leading man from lynch lika that is old as he'sa fren' Methuselah! He'sa want something new for finish that picture—bran' new, he'sa holler or no picture! All morning I worka, worka, worka, he'sa maka faces at everything I do!"

"Well!" I says. "If you—"

I happened to look up just then and I seen the well known gates of Film City about a hundred yards away, and if we was makin' a mile an hour, we was makin' fifty. I leaned over and tapped the Kid on the shoulder.

"Don't you think you had better slow up a trifle?" I asks him.

"I don't *think* nothin' about it!" he throws over his shoulder. "I *know* it! I been tryin' to stop this thing for the last fifteen minutes and there's nothin' doin'!"

"Throw her in reverse!" I screams, as them great big iron gates looms up over the front mud guards.

"I can't!" he shouts. "The darned thing's stuck in high and I can't budge it!"

One of them gates was open and the Kid steers for it, while I closed my eyes and give myself over to prayer. We shot through leavin' one lamp, both mudguards and a runnin' board behind.

"Hey!" yells Genaro. "What's a mat? Thisa too fasta for me! Stoppa the car before something she'sa happen!"

"Somethin' she'sa gonna happen right now!" I says. "Be seated!"

The Kid swings around a corner and everybody in Film City is either lookin', runnin' or yellin' after us. I often wondered what a wide berth meant, and I found out that afternoon. That's what everybody in the place give us when we come through there hittin' on six as I. Markowitz would remark. A guy made up like a Indian chief jumped behind a tree and we only missed him by dumb luck.

"Hey!" he yells after us. "Are you fellows crazy? Look out for the Moorish Castle!"

I yelled back that we wouldn't miss nothin' of interest, if we could help it and the gas held out, and just then I got a flash at the Moorish Castle. It had been built the day before for a big five reel thriller that Genaro was gonna produce and I understand he was very partial to it. As soon as he sees it he jumps up in the back of the car and slaps the Kid on the shoulders.

"Hey, crazee man!" he hollers. "Stoppa the car, I, Genaro, command it! Don't toucha my castle!" his voice goes off in a shriek. "*Sapristi!* — I — "

That was all he said just then, because we went through the Moorish Castle like a cyclone through Kansas, and as we come out on the other side the whole thing tumbled down, bringin' with it a couple of Chinese pagodas that had just come from the paint shop. All we lost was half of the radiator and the windshield. The Kid pulls a kind of a sick grin and licks his lips.

"Some car, eh?" he says, takin' a fresh grip on the steerin' wheel.

I missed Genaro and lookin' back through the dust I seen him draped over a fence with his head touchin' the ground and his feet up in the air. A lot of daredevils was runnin' towards us and yellin' murder.

"Where's Genaro?" asks the Kid, as we miss a tree by a half inch.

I shivered and told him.

"The big quitter!" snarls the Kid. "Left us flat the minute somethin' happened, eh? I always knew that guy was yellah!"

We shot across the African Desert and comin' around another turn we bust right into "The Escapes of Eva." There's about two hundred supers dressed like cowboys and Duke, Genaro's assistant, is up on a little platform with the Big Boss Potts, directin' the thing. De Vronde is under a tree with a rope around his neck and another one that don't show in the picture under his arms so's he can be pulled up and it will look like he was bein' lynched. A little ways up the road is Miss Vincent on a horse, ready to make her dash to save De Vronde's life.

As all this comes into view, the Kid swings around on me and shoves somethin' big and round in my face.

"Now!" he hollers. "We're up against it for real! The steerin' wheel come off!"

I pushed open the door on the side and stood on the runnin' board.

"Let me know how you make out!" I yells. "I got enough!"

With that I jumps.

Just as I hit the ground, I hear Duke yellin' through a megaphone.

"C'mon, now—gimme action! Hey! Get two of those cameras at an angle. When I say 'Shoot!' you, Nelson, and Hardy pull that rope so De Vronde swings about five feet clear of the ground! Be sure the rope is under his arms, too! Hey, you extra people—a little ginger there! This is a lynching not a spelling bee! Dance around some—yell! That's it. Now, all ready?" He blows the whistle. "Shoot!" he yells, "and gimme all you got!"

Well, the Kid did what he could—he blowed the little trick horn on the side of the car about a second before he shot into the mob. Them bloodthirsty outlaws just melted away before him, and them that was slow-witted was picked up and tossed to one side before they knowed what hit 'em. They's a big stone wall at the other side of the tree and that's where the Kid was headed for. Just as he sails under De Vronde, who's hangin' from the rope over his head, the Kid sees the wall, grabs De Vronde by the legs and hangs there, lettin' that crazy, six cylinder A. G. F. proceed without him. De Vronde and the Kid crashes to the ground and the car dashed its brains out against the wall.

While great excitement is bein' had by all, Duke jumps from the platform to tell the camera men to cease firin' and a handful of actors runs over to jimmy the Kid and De Vronde apart. I thought this Duke guy was gonna explode, on the level it was two minutes before he could speak.

"What d'ye mean, you ivory-headed simp?" he screams at the Kid, finally. "What d'ye mean by that? You've ruined a hundred feet of film, you—"

I hear somebody puffin' along beside me as I come runnin' up and I see it's Potts. He's red in the face and mumblin' somethin' to himself as he waddles along. I felt real sorry for the Kid—car and job, both gone! Potts rushes up and grabs Duke by the shoulder.

"There!" he yells, pointin' to the Kid. "There stands a man that knows more about the picture game than the whole infernal lot of you! *That's the kind of a finish I've been trying to get for this picture all morning*!"

CHAPTER III
PLEASURE ISLAND

Speakin' of boobs, as people will, did you ever figure what would happen if the production of 'em would suddenly cease? Heh? Where would this or any other country be, if all the voters was wise guys and the suckers was all dead?

In the first place, there wouldn't have been no ex-Land of the Rave and Home of the Spree, if Queen Isabella hadn't been boob enough to fall for Columbus's stuff, about would she stake him and his gang of rough and readys to a couple of ferryboats and they'd go out and bring back Chicago. Even old Chris himself was looked on as Kid Stupid, because he claimed the earth was round. The gang he trailed with had it figured as bein' square like their heads.

The guy that invented the airship was doped out as a boob until the thing begin to fly, the bird that turned out the first steamboat was called a potterin' old simp and let him alone and he'd kill himself—and that's the way it goes.

The sucker is the boy that keeps the wise guys alive. He'll try anything once, and it don't make no difference to him whether it's three-card monte or a new kind of submarine. He's the guy that built all the fancy bridges, the big buildin's, fought and won the wars that the wise guys started, and fixed things generally so that to-day you can push a little trick electric button and get anything from a piece of pie to a divorce. He's the simp that falls for the new minin' company stock, grins when the wise guys explain to him just how many kinds of a sucker he is, and then clips coupons while *they're* gettin' up early to read the want ads. He's the baby that's done everything that couldn't be did.

That's the boob!

The boob is the guy that takes all the chances and makes it possible for old Kid World to keep goin' forward instead of standin' still. Any burg that's got a couple of sure enough eighteen-carat boobs in it, known to the trade as suckers, has got a chance.

So the next time somebody calls you a big boob, don't get sore—thank him. He's boostin' you!

Gimme ten boobs in back of me and I'll take a town, because they'll take a chance. Gimme a hundred wise guys and the town'll take *us*, because them birds will have to stop and figure what's the use of startin' somethin'.

Me for the boobs!

Kid Scanlan was a boob. He was a great battler, a regular fellow and all like that, but he was a boob just the same. He started fightin' because he was simp enough to take a chance of havin' his features altered, and he won the title through bein' stupid enough to mix it with the welterweight champion. I was the wise guy of the party, always playin' it safe and seein' what made it go, before I'd take a chance. But the Kid got a whole lot further than I ever will. He made a name for himself in the ring and another in the movies and I ain't champion of *nothin'*—I'm just *with* Scanlan, that's all.

I'm gettin' offers from promoters here and there to have him start against some set up for money that was sinful to refuse, but there's nothin' doin'. The Kid has took to bein' an actor like they did to gunpowder in Europe, and not only he won't fight, I can't even get him mad!

"I'm off that roughneck stuff!" he tells me. "Nobody ever got nothin' by fightin'. Look what it did to Willard! Besides," he goes on, "what would John Drew and them guys think of me, if it should leak out that I had give in to box fightin' again? Why they'd be off me for life! Nope, let 'em battle in Russia, I'm through!"

Fine for a champion, eh?

Now here's a guy that went to the top in the one game where you can't luck your way over. Because he was a fightin' fool, the 'Kid had right-crossed his way to the title and now that he was up there, the big stiff wouldn't look at a glove! No! he was a actor now! I'd tell him that Kid Whosthis had flattened Battlin' McGluke the night before and we could get ten thousand to go six rounds with the winner. He'd flick the ash off a gold-tipped cigarette and say,

"Yeh?" Then he'd grab me by the shoulder and pour this in my ear. "Did you get me in that Shakespeare picture last week? I hear the guy that writes up shows for the Peoria *Gazette* claims Mansfield had nothin' on me!"

A few months before he would have said somethin' like this,

"All right! Wire the club we'll fight him, and if I don't bounce that tramp in two rounds, I'll give my end to them starvin' Armenians!"

Now I didn't kick when the Kid falls for Miss Vincent, because I had seen Miss Vincent, and the Kid was only human. I didn't say nothin' when he staked himself to that second-hand auto that like to wrecked California, but when he pulls this actor thing on me and says pugilism, *pugilism*, mind you, ought to be discouraged—I figured it was about time for yours in the faith to step in.

The Kid had two ambitions in life, both of which he picked up at Film City. One was to be the greatest movie hero that ever flattened a villain, and the other was to ease himself into the Golden West Club.

The Golden West Club was over in Frisco, and as far as the average guy was concerned it could have been in Iceland. It was about as easy to get into that joint as it is to get into Heaven, and it was also the only other place where you couldn't buy your way in. Your name had to be Fortescue-Smith or Van Whosthis, and you had to look it. You had to be partial to tea, wrist watches, dancin', opera, tennis and the like, and to top it all off you had to be a distant relative to a hick called William the Conqueror, who I hear was light heavy-weight champ in days of old. If you checked up all right on them little details, they took a vote on you. If you was lucky, you got a letter in a few weeks later sayin' your application was bein' considered and you might get in, but not to bank on it, because they was havin' trouble connectin' up your grandfather with the rest of the family tree, it bein' said around that he made his money through work.

That was the place Kid Scanlan wanted to bust into!

One night he gets all dressed up like a horse in one of them soup and fish layouts, and he hires a guy to drive him over to the Golden West Club in that second-hand A. G. F. he had. I will say the Kid went into the thing in a big way, payin' seventy-five bucks for a dress suit and ten more for the whitest shirt I ever seen in my life. He sends in eight berries for a hack-driver's hat and seven for a pair of tan shoes. Then he climbs into his bus and tells the driver, "Let's go!" Before he pulled out, he told me they was so many guys belonged to the thing that he figured he could mix around for a few minutes without anybody gettin' wise that he wasn't a regular member, if he could only breeze past the jobbie on the door.

And outside of the shoes, which I thought was a trifle noisy, the Kid sized up like any of the real club members I had seen, except his chest wasn't so narrow and he had an intelligent look.

Well, he blowed in about twelve o'clock and come up to the rooms we had at the hotel in Film City. He stands in the middle of the bedroom, takes off this trick silk hat, and, puttin' everything he had on the throw, he pitched it into the bathtub. He slammed that open-faced coat in a corner and in a minute it was followed by them full-dress pants. The gleamin' white shirt skidded under the bed, neck and neck with the shoes. I didn't say a word while he was abusin' them clothes, but I was so happy I felt like cheerin', because they was somethin' in the Kid's face I hadn't seen there since we hit the movies. The last time I had caught him lookin' like that was when One-Punch Ross had dropped him with a left hook, just before the Kid won the title.

When the Kid got to his feet that there look was on his face and two seconds later he was welterweight champion of the world and points adjacent.

He inserts himself into his pyjamas and then he swings around on me.

"How much did they offer us at the Garden for ten rounds with Battlin' Edwards?" he wants to know.

I liked to fell out of the bed!

"Eight thousand, with a privilege of thirty per cent of the gross," I says, gettin' off of the hay. "Will I wire 'em?"

"Yep!" he snaps out. "Tell 'em I'll fight Edwards two weeks after I get through here!"

"And when will that be, might I ask?" I says, ringin' for a messenger and tryin' to keep from dancin' a jig.

"As soon as them simps finish that picture, 'How Kid Scanlan Won the Title,'" he tells me. "Genaro says he'll start it to-morrow, and as soon as it's through, so am I—here!"

I didn't get the answer to all this until the Kid crawls into the hay half a hour later, scowlin' and mutterin' to himself. I took a good look at him and then I says,

"Speakin' of clubs and stuff like that, how did you make out at that Golden West joint to-night?"

He sits right up in the bed.

"Are you tryin' to kid somebody?" he snarls.

"I asked you a civil question, you big stiff!" I comes back, "and don't be comin' around here and slippin' *me* that rough stuff! If you can be a gentleman at your clubs and joints like that, you want to be one here! D'ye get that?"

He looks at me for a minute and seein' I'm serious, he growls,

"I thought you had heard about it!" Then he props himself up with the pillows and begins, "I went over there to-night and them boobs was havin' a racket of some kind, I guess, because all the automobiles in the West was lined up outside the doors of the club. I tried to horn in the line with that boat of mine and the biggest nigger in the world, dressed up like a band leader, comes over and wants to know if I'm a guest. I told him no, that I was a movie actor and to step one side or he'd break the headlights when I hit him. He claims I can't get in the line without I got a ticket showin' I'm a guest. I got tired of his chatter, so I dropped him with a short left swing and we keep on goin' till we wind up at the front door. This stupid simp I had drivin' my bus is lookin' at the swell dames goin' in, instead of at the emergency brake, and he forgets to stop the thing till we have took off the rear end of a car in front of us and busted my front mudguard again.

"While the chiffure of the wreck is moanin' to my guy about it, I ducked out the side and blowed around to the entrance. I figured they was a password of some kind, so I says to the big hick at the gate, 'Ephus Doffus Loffus,' and pushes past him, I guess he was surprised at me bein' a stranger and knowin' the ropes at that, because I seen him lookin' after me when I beat it up the first stairway to the second floor. I got a flash at myself in a mirror as I breeze past, and, if I do say it myself, I was there forty ways. I was simply a knockout in that evenin' dress thing! A swell-lookin' guy pipes me at the top of the stairs and, after givin' me the once over, he taps me on the arm.

"'You may bring me a glawss of Appollinaris, my man,' he says, 'and for heaven sake remove those yellow shoes!'

"With that he walks away and another guy comes up and whistles at me. When I turn around, he's givin' me the up and down through a glass thing he's got hung over one eye.

"'Bring up a box of perfectos at once!' he pipes. 'Come! Look alive now!'

"Then I got it! *I* thought I was knockin' 'em dead and these guys thought I was a waiter! Well, I thinks, I'll show them boobs somethin' before I take the air—I can pull that stuff *myself*! With that I breezes into the next room and there's a hick sittin' at a table, toyin' with a book. He was as near nothin' as anything I ever seen, on the level! He's got a swell dress suit on, but it didn't fit him no better than mine did me and it couldn't have cost no more or he would have killed the tailor. Outside of the shoes, mine bein' classier, we was both made up the same. A guy comes in, looks him over for a minute and then he yawns. 'Bored?' he says. The simp that was sittin' down looks back at him, yawns and says, 'Frightfully.' Then the other guy bows at him and goes out. Some other hick wanders in and says, 'Ah, Van Stuyvessant, bored?' and Stupid says, 'Frightfully' and the other guy blows out. I seen that the coast was clear, so I smoothed my hair, pulled down my vest and throwed my chest out like them other guys did. Then I breezed in and stopped before this guy. He yawns and looks up at me very dignified like he was sittin' in the Night Court and I was up before him for the third time in a week.

"'Hey, Stupid!' I says. 'Get me a gin fizz and don't make it too sweet! And for heaven's sakes get rid of that shirt!'

"I thought he was goin' to get the apoplexy or somethin', because his face is as red as a four-alarm fire. Then he says,

"'Why—what—how dare you, you insolent puppy!'

"I leaned on his shoulder and tapped him on the end of the beak with my thumb.

"'Lay off that stuff, Simple,' I tells him. 'I'm a guest here and a couple of hicks took me for a waiter. I'm just gettin' even, that's all. If you don't get me that gin fizz like I asked you, I'll knock you for a goal!'

"He gets as white as my shirt and presses a little button on the table. A big husky, made up like a Winter Garden chorus man, runs in and Stupid says, 'Eject this ruffian, Simms! And then you will answer to me for allowing him to enter!'

"Simms was game, but a poor worker, so I feinted him over in front of his master and then I flattened him with a left and right to the jaw. I took it on the run then and got out the back way!"

The Kid stops and heaves a sigh.

"And then what?" I encourages him.

"And then nothin'!" he says. "That's all! Except I'm off the Golden West Club, the movies and this part of the country! I got enough. Them guys over there to-night gimme the tip-off—I don't belong, that's all! I was a sucker to ever stop fightin' to be a actor, but I got wise in time. You go ahead and sign me right up with anybody but Dempsey, and if Genaro don't start my picture to-morrow, I'll give 'em back their money and you and me will leave the Golden West flat on its back!"

Say! I was so happy I couldn't sleep. I just turned over on my side and registered joy all night long!

The next mornin' we go to Genaro the first thing, and the Kid puts it up to him right off the bat. Either he starts "How Kid Scanlan Won the Title" or he kisses us good-by. Genaro raves and pulls his hair for awhile, but they ain't no more give to the Kid than they is to marble and finally Genaro says he'll start the picture right away.

We find out that another director is usin' the whole camp to put on a trick called "The Fall of Babylon," so we got to go over to an island in the well known Pacific Ocean and take what they call exteriors there. They rounded up Miss Vincent, De Vronde, the cuckoo that wrote the thing, and about a hundred other people and load us all on a yacht belongin' to Potts. We're gonna stay on this trick island till the picture is finished, and we eat and sleep on the yacht.

On the trip over, we all go down in what Potts claims is the grand saloon and Van Aylstyne, the hick that wrote the picture, reads it to us. It starts off showin' the Kid workin' in a pickle factory on the East Side in New York. They're only slippin' him five berries a week and out of that he's keepin' his widowed mother and seven of her children. One day he finds a newspaper and all over the front page is a article tellin' about all the money the welterweight champion is makin', so the Kid figures the pickle game is no place for a young feller with his talent, and decides to become welterweight champ. First he tries himself out by slammin' the guy he's workin' for, after catchin' him insultin' the stenographer by askin' her to take a ride in his runabout, when the buyer is already takin' her out in his limousine. When the boss comes back to life, he fires the Kid and our hero goes out and knocks down a few odd brutes here and there for gettin' fresh with innocent chorus girls and the like. Finally, he practically wrecks a swell gamblin' joint where he has gone to rescue his girl, which had been lured there by the handsome stranger from the city.

"Well!" says Potts, when Van Aylstyne gets finished. "How does that strike you?"

"What I like," pipes Miss Vincent, with a funny little quirk of her lip and a wink at De Vronde. "What I like is its daring originality!"

Van Aylstyne stiffens up.

"Of course," he says, kinda sore, "if I'm to be criticised by—"

"Ain't they no villains or nothin' like that in it?" butts in the Kid, frownin' at him.

"Joosta one minoote!" says Genaro. "Don't get excite! That's joosta firsta reel!"

He waves his hand at Van Aylstyne, and this guy gives a couple of glares all around and then turns over another page. It seems at this stage of the game, a lot of gunmen get together to stop the Kid from winnin' the title, so they throw him off a cliff. He gets up, dusts off his clothes, registers anger and flattens half a dozen of 'em. A little bit later he gets fastened to a railroad track and the fast mail runs over him. This makes him peeved, and he gets up and wallops a couple of tramps that's passing for luck. Then the villain's gang of rough and readys grabs him again and he is throwed off a ship into the ocean. A guy comes along in a motor boat, and, after shootin' a few times at the Kid without actually killin' him, registers surprise and runs over him. When the Kid comes up there ain't nothin' to wallop, so he swims six miles to the island. The minute he crawls on the beach he faces the camera and registers exhaustion. Then a lot of guys jump out and stab him. He knocks 'em all cold and then he goes on, fights the champ and wins the title.

"Is that all there is to it?" asks the Kid, when Van Aylstyne stops for breath and applause.

"Practically all," Van Aylstyne tells him. "Of course I'll have to go over it and spice it up a little more—get more action in it here and there, wherever it appears to drag. But we can do this as we go along."

"Yes!" says Potts. "You'll have to do that. I want this picture to be the thriller of the year!" He scratches his chin for a minute and looks at Van Aylstyne. "You better ginger it up a bit at that!" he goes on. "It sounds a little tame to me. See if you can't work in a couple of spectacular fires, a sensational runaway with Mr. Scanlan being dragged along the ground, or you might have him do a slide for life from the topmast of the yacht to one of the trees along the shore here."

"Wait!" pipes Genaro. "I have joosta the thing! While I listen, I getta thisa granda idea! Meester Scanlan, he'sa can be throw from the airsheep and—"

"Lay off, lay off!" butts in the 'Kid. "They's enough action in that thing right now to suit me! Don't put nothin' else in it. I'll be busier than a one-armed paperhanger as it is!" He turns to Van Aylstyne. "Where d'ye get that stuff?" he scowls. "Would *you* jump off a cliff, hey?"

Van Aylstyne throws out his little chest, while the rest of them snickers.

"I *write* it!" he says.

"Yeh?" pipes the Kid. "Well, you'll *jump* it, too, bo,

believe me!"

"What's a mat?" hollers Genaro. "What's a use hava the fighta now? Wait till we starta the picture, then everybody she'sa fighta! Something she'sa go wrong. *Sapristi*! we feexa her then. Joosta holda tight your horses!"

He pats the Kid on the shoulder and slips him a cigar.

The rest of the trip to the island took about two hours, durin' which time the Kid and Miss Vincent sat on the top deck, and she give him his daily lesson in how to speak English, eat soup and a lot more of that high society stuff.

We finally got to this island place and by three o'clock the next afternoon they was half way through with the first reel. I horned in on the thing myself, takin' off a copper, for which they gimme five bucks even.

That night they was big doings on board the yacht. They had music and dancin' and what not galore. Van Aylstyne, Potts, De Vronde and most of the other help was there in the soup and fish and the twenty odd dames that was actin' in the picture was all dressed up to thrill. I never seen so much of this here de collect stuff in my life. I heard a lot of talk around the studios at the camp about "exposures," and, well, I seen what they meant all right that evenin'. It got me so dizzy, never havin' no closeups like that before, that I ducked for my stateroom about nine o'clock when the joy was just beginnin' to be unconfined and I hadn't been up there five minutes, when the Kid comes up and knocks at my door.

"I'm goin' to hit the hay," he tells me. "If I gotta fight Battlin' Edwards in two months, I'm gonna start readyin' up now! I been puttin' on fat since I been here, and it's got to come off. I'll get up at five to-morrow and do a gallop around the island, and I just dug up a couple of ex-bartenders among the extry people which will gimme some sparrin' practice every mornin' till they give out!"

"Great!" I says. I was hardly able to believe my ears. It

sounded like the old Kid Scanlan again!

I closed the door, and just as he was turnin' away, I heard the swish of skirts and then I got Miss Vincent's voice. It was low and sweet and kinda soothin' and—well, she was the kind of dame guys kill each other for! Do you get me?

"Oh!" she kinda breathes. "Why are you up here all alone?"

I heard the Kid's deep breathin'—it was always that way when *she* spoke to him, and I knowed without seein' 'em that his nails was engravin' fancy work on the palm of his hand.

"Why," he says, tryin' to keep his voice steady. "I'm off this tango thing—and the last time I had one of them dress suits on, I was mistook for a waiter!"

Y'know there was a funny little catch in the Kid's voice when he pulled that, although he tried to pass it off by coughin'. That boy sure did want to mix with the big leaguers, and, bein' Irish, it come hard to him to miss anything he wanted. Usually he got it!

I heard Miss Vincent sneer.

"Don't flatter these conceit-drugged travesties on the male sex by caring about anything *they* say," she tells him. "You have so many things they never will have! Why, you're a big, clean, two-handed man and—" She breaks off and gives a giggle that I would have took Verdun for. "But there!" she goes on. "I—I—guess I'm getting too enthusiastic!"

I could almost feel her blush, and I knowed how she looked when she did that thing, so I says, "Good-by, Kid!"

"That's all right!" pipes the Kid. "It wasn't these guys here. But I can't go downstairs anyhow, because I gotta start trainin' for Battlin' Edwards."

"Oh, bother Battling Edwards!" she says. "I thought you promised me to give up prize fighting!"

This was a new one on me, and it cleared up a lot of things I hadn't been able to figure out before!

"I gotta take it back," I hear the Kid sayin' in a kinda dead voice. "I pulled a bone play when I did that! I can't give up fightin' no more than you can give up the movies! The only thing I got is a wallop, and that won't get me nowhere in the movies or society, but it got me the title in the ring. I guess I'll stick to my own game!"

"Oh, come!" she tells him, kinda impatient. "You have the blues! Shake 'em off—I don't like you when you scowl like that. Come on down and have a dance with me. You'll feel better."

"You said somethin'!" answers the Kid. "But I can't—on the level. I gotta train for this guy, or he's liable to bounce me, and, if I lose this quarrel, I'm through! Y'see, this ain't no movie, this is gonna be the real thing! If this guy flattens me, he'll be the champion and you *know* that bird is gonna be in there tryin' till the last bell!"

I peeked through them little wooden cheaters on the window and I seen her kinda stiffen up and register surprise.

"I am not accustomed to coaxing people to dance with me, Mr. Scanlan," she says, "and—"

"Yes, and I'm not used to havin' dames like *you* ask me!" butts in the Kid. "But I gotta beat Edwards—and I can't beat him by stayin' up late!"

She just breezes past him and down the deck without another word.

The Kid kicks a fire bucket that was standin' there into the Pacific Ocean, and from the way he slammed the door of his stateroom I'll bet all them trick beer mugs that Potts had on the wall fell on the floor.

Well, the next mornin' we all go over to the island again and the Kid is up at daybreak, trottin' over the hills. He's got four sweaters on, although it's as hot as blazes, and I'm taggin' along in back of him. Then he comes back, changes his clothes and works in the picture till noon, when we knock off for the eats. Miss Vincent passed us once when we was talkin' to Genaro, and she deliberately passed the Kid up!

After that it was suicide to give Scanlan a nasty look.

Along around two o'clock that afternoon, another yacht shows up a little ways off the island and in a few minutes it stops and five guys and a woman hops in one of them trick launches and put-puts over to us. They get out and come up the string-piece and we get a good flash at them. The male members of the party is all dressed up in blue coats and white pants and from their general get-up I thought they was all gonna form a circle, pick up the ends of their coats and pipe. "What ho, the merry villagers come and we are the daisy maids!"

All but one. He was a great big husky, kinda dark skinned and he looked like a assassin with the women, know what I mean? Also, I had seen this bird somewheres before, but I couldn't check him up right off the bat. The girl that was with the troupe was a good looker all right, and you could see she was a big-timer. But she was kinda thin and worn out to the naked eye. And when I got a close-up of her, I seen there was a funny look in her eyes, like she had been double-crossed or somethin'. She looked at everything like she wished it was hers, but there was no chance, d'ye get me?

Well, Potts comes a-runnin' to meet 'em and then he comes up and introduces 'em all around. He claims they're from Frisco and friends of his which has come over to see how movin' pictures is made and they might even go so far as to take off a part in one of 'em, just for the devilment of it. Miss Vincent looks hard and close at the dark-skinned guy, like she was tryin' to think where she had seen him before, but Genaro come along just then and I'll bet them newcomers didn't get no encouragement from the way *he* looked 'em over. De Vronde and Van Aylstyne, though, fell for this bunch so hard they liked to broke their necks. It seems them two hicks found out they all was members of this Golden West Club, and they did everything but shine their shoes from then on.

When the Kid blows in and sees 'em, he claims he remembers 'em all as bein' among them present the night he went over to the Club, and he says they had better keep lots of the Golden West between him and them while they was in our midst.

The tall dark guy, whose name was somethin' like Brown-Smith, took one flash at Miss Vincent and then everybody else could have been in France for all the notice *he* give 'em. He took up his stand about two feet away from her, and there he stuck all day long like cement. Anybody could see that this stuff was causin' two people to register worry. They was the Kid and the dame that come over with the troupe. Scanlan watches Brown-Smith makin' his play for Miss Vincent, and he seen that if she wasn't encouragin' him, she wasn't complainin' to the police either, but the Kid keeps quiet and takes it out in makin' them sparrin' ex-bartenders tired of life.

The next day I got up early lookin' for the Kid, and as I come through a clearin' in the island I seen three things at once, and if I hadn't ducked behind a tree, they'd have seen me. There's my meal ticket with all his sweaters off, standin' in the middle of the little space, shadow boxin' in front of a tree. The well known sun is shinin' down on his blonde head, and I never noticed before just what a handsome brute the Kid was in action. The muscles in his arms are jumpin' and ripplin' under a skin that a chorus girl would give five years for, and he's as graceful and light on his feet as one of them Russian toe dancers.

The other two things I seen was Miss Vincent and the dame that had blowed in with the Golden West boys.

The new dame is watchin' the Kid like he was a most pleasin' sight to them tired little eyes of hers. Her mouth is open a little bit and there's a kind of wishin' smile on her lips. Y'know she looked like this was what she wanted ever since she come into the store. Get me?

Miss Vincent is doin' a piece of watchin' herself around the tree that's between 'em, only she ain't watchin' the Kid. She's watchin' this new dame, and you can take it from me she was registerin' hate! That classy little nose of hers is quiverin' and she's bitin' hard on her lip. Her body was so stiff and straight that, on the level, I thought she was gonna spring!

The Kid finally stops boxin', puts on his sweaters and then he gets a flash at the new dame. She calls somethin' to him and he comes over—then they start back to the yacht together. Miss Vincent ducks and so did I. I didn't want *none* of them to see me, because this thing was gettin' a little too deep for yours in the faith.

They go ahead with another reel of the Kid's picture that morning and Brown-Smith still keeps hangin' around Miss Vincent like a panhandler outside a circus, and when she has to come in the picture herself, he stands on the sidelines beside one of the camera men, with them chorus men friends of his draped around him. The Kid is goin' through a scene where he flattens half a dozen guys that are tryin' to discourage him from fightin' the champ and Brown-Smith is givin' his friends the low down on it.

"By Jove!" he sneers, just loud enough so's we can all get an earful. "It nauseates me to see that fellow knocking about those poor devils who have to do that for a living! Fawncy him doing anything like that in real life! Why, he would most likely call for the police if some one slapped his wrist. I know those moving picture heroes!"

This troupe of Sweet Williams around him snickers right out loud in public at that, like the big guy was simply a knockout as a comedian. Miss Vincent frowns and the new dame looks kinda worried and nervous, but the Kid just reddens a bit and continues to swat the supers all over the lot. Brown-Smith pulls a few more raw cracks like that, gettin' louder and nastier all the time, and finally he asks Potts to let him take part in the big scene at the end of the reel where the Kid is supposed to bounce everybody in the thing but the camera men. He says it will be great stuff to tell about at the club the first rainy night and a lot of bunk like that—all the time he's watchin' the Kid with that nasty sneer on his face.

Potts says all right, and offers to stake him to an old suit of clothes, but he laughs and says he won't need anything, tossin' his coat to one side like the acrobat at the theatre flips away his handkerchief before goin' to work. He rolls up his sleeves and starts limberin' up his arms in front of Miss Vincent, winkin' at her and noddin' to the Kid. She looks kinda worried, but her control is good and she holds fast. She wasn't the only one that looked worried, believe me! I was doin' that thing myself, because this Brown-Smith guy had a good thirty pounds on the Kid, and he was built that way all over, reach, height and everything else. The minute he put up his hands, I seen two things. First, that he knowed somethin' about box fightin' and, second, that he was goin' to try and bounce the Kid for the benefit of Miss Vincent.

While they're gettin' things ready for the massacre, the Kid comes over to me and says,

"What's the big idea? I know this bird—he's the guy that asked me to bring him a *glawss* of Appollinaris that night at the Golden West Club. If he fusses around me, I'm gonna maul him!"

I knowed *that* wasn't the reason, because Kid Scanlan could take both a wallop or a joke. The reason was standin' about three feet away talkin' to Genaro and she never looked better. Believe me, she had everything that mornin'!

"Looka thisa bigga boob, Miss Vincent!" Genaro is sayin', wavin' his arms around and shakin' his head at Brown-Smith. "He'sa wanna get in my picture so he showa the girls what a bigga fella he is. Meester Potts he's a go crazee if thisa picture she's a no good. He's a joomp at me, he's a holler at me and he letta thisa bigga bunk get in it! Thisa fight, she'sa gotta looka real—not lika the actor, butta *real*! Thisa fella he'sa go in slappa Meester Scanlan on he'sa wrist. Meester Scanlan he'sa no wanna hurt Meester Potts' fren'—you know?—so he'sa slappa heem back! Everybody she'sa laugh at me when they showa that picture. Aha! They maka me crazee!"

He runs over to Brown-Smith and grabs his arm.

"Please, Meester!" he begs him, with tears in his eyes. "Please, Meester, getta gooda and rough with thisa fella!" he points to the Kid. "Don't be afraid for heem, he's a tougha nut! He's a nevaire geta hurt! Don't maka thisa fight looka like the act. You rusha heem, hitta heem, wrestle heem, choka heem, graba heem, bita heem, kicka heem, anything but keela heem, so thisa picture she looka like reala fight! Pretty soon, I blowa the whistle. He's a hitta you easy—so—you falla down. Maka looka good, don't sitta down, falla down—so!—" Genaro stops and throws himself on the grass and then hops up again. "You watcha that?" he goes on. "Alla right!" He jumps away from the cameras and yells, "Hey, Joe! You stanna over there and shoota this froma the right! Alla right, now everybody! Meester Kid Scanlan, you ready? Gooda! Come now—cameras—ready— shoot!"

The Kid meets the rush of the gang like they had practised it together, and he floors one after the other of them with snappy left hooks. Of course he was pullin' his punches and barely touchin' these hicks, but it looked awful good from front. Then Brown-Smith, who had been hangin' around on the outside, rushes in. For a guy who had never tried the thing before, he struck me as bein' real swift at pickin' up the rules, because he faced the cameras at the right angles and pulled a lot of fancy stuff that usually nobody but a sure enough movie actor knows. The Kid sidesteps him and puts a light left to his chin and Brown-Smith comes back with a right swing that would have floored the Kid, if it hadn't been too high. The Kid went back on his heels and a little trickle of claret comes from his lips. Genaro jumps in the air, clappin' his hands. "Magnificenta!" he yells. Miss Vincent is breathin' hard and her hands pressed up tight against her chest. Her face was the color of skimmed milk. Genaro pipes her and grabs a camera man. "Shoota that— queek!" he hollers, pointin' to her. The new dame runs over to me and grabs my arm.

"Stop it!" she whispers, excited like. "You must! Albert will kill him! He was amateur heavyweight champion once and —oh!—he wants to beat Mr. Scanlan—he—oh!—"

I heard Miss Vincent give a little yelp, and I shove this dame away and, believe me, bo, *I* come near goin' dead on my feet! *Because there's my champ on the ground, layin' flat on his face and he looked as cold as the North Pole!* I started to dash in, but Genaro grabs me and throws me aside. "Stoppa, fool!" he yells. "Thisa picture she'sa maka me famous!"

The rest of the mob is too scared to do anything—they knowed that this was the real thing! The Kid gets up on one knee, and, on the level, the only sound you could hear was his choked breathin' and the steady click of the cameras—yes, and I guess the beatin' of my heart! The Kid is shakin' his head to clear it from that wallop and I yelled to him to stay down and take his time. He gets half way up and slides down again flat and Brown-Smith laughs. Then Miss Vincent suddenly turns, and there's a bucket of ice cold lemonade standin' on a bench beside her. It had been put there for the extry people. This here eighteen-carat, regular fellow dame grabs that bucket and throws the lemonade all over the Kid's head and shoulders!

It braced him like a charge of hop—his head jerked up as it hit him and he shook off the drops—and in another second he was on his feet, smilin' the old Scanlan smile and dancin' around this guy who was rushin' in to finish him. He swings for the Kid's jaw and the Kid, movin' his head an inch out of the way, puts a hard right and left to the mouth. Brown-Smith coughed

out a tooth that he had no further use for, and starts backin'
away, coverin' up like a crab. The Kid laughs over at me and
sends this guy's head back like it was on a hinge, with two
uppercuts and a right jab. He tries to rush in and grab the Kid,
and Scanlan closes his left eye with the prettiest straight left I
ever seen. He wasn't tryin' to knock this big stiff out, he was
deliberately cuttin' him to pieces in a most cold, workmanlike
manner.

Miss Vincent is smilin' now and the other dame—is not!
Potts's mouth is open about five yards and he looks like he don't
know whether to call the police or go back to the box office for a
better seat. Then the Kid starts backin' friend Brown-Smith all
over the place, shootin' lefts and rights at him so fast that I bet he
thought it was rainin' wallops. He begins to register yellah—he
gazes around wildly at Genaro and Genaro reaches for the
whistle so's Brown-Smith can quit, but Miss Vincent sees him
reach for it and she knocks it out of his hand! Genaro looks hard
at her and yells to the camera men to keep turnin' the cranks.
Potts starts over, stops, shakes his shoulders and turns his back.

Then the Kid tips back Brown-Smith's head with a
lightnin' right hook and drops him with a left to the jaw.

They stopped the cameras and everybody give a hand in
bringin' the dashin' Brown-Smith back to the Golden West
again. Everybody but me, the Kid and Miss Vincent. The Kid
walks over to Potts and stares at him.

"Well," he says. "I guess I'm through after that, eh?"

Potts slaps him on the back.

"Hardly!" he grins. "That was the greatest piece of acting
I ever saw before a camera!"

Genaro runs up and grabs the Kid's hand.

"Wonderful!" he hollers. "Magnificenta! You are what
you calla the true artiste, Meester Kid Scanlan! That picture she
will be the talka of the country! She'sa maka me famous!"

"Yeh?" says the Kid. He turns to me and waves over to

where Brown-Smith is recognizin' relatives and close friends. "That guy has an awful good left!" he says. He thinks for a minute. "D'ye know," he goes on, "that hick was *tryin'*, at that!"

I see Miss Vincent talkin' to Potts and all of a sudden he throws up his hands and stares over at Brown-Smith.

"What?" he hollers. "Impossible!"

Then he slaps his hands together and laughs out loud.

"Oh!" he says, holdin' his sides. "This is too much! Ha, ha, ha!"

"What's the joke?" I asks Miss Vincent.

"It's more of a tragedy!" she says, kinda hysterical like she was glad it was all over. "That man is no more Brown-Smith than you are. He's Albert Ellington LaRue, who five years ago was the biggest moving picture leading man in the country! Why, he got hundreds of letters every day from poor, foolish little girls who grew dizzy watching him foil villains in five reels a week. He inherited some money—quite a lot, I believe, and suddenly vanished from the screen, turning up as Brown-Smith here last year. But he simply could not resist the call of his vanity to come back once more as the dashing hero of the film. He had planned to step into this picture, turn the tables in the fight with Mr. Scanlan, who he thought was an actor and not a pugilist, and thus come back to the movies in a blaze of glory! He told me he had two press agents awaiting the word to flash his coup all over the country. He thought it would make a great story!" She stopped and laughed. "It will!" she goes on. "Think of the matinée girls when they see their darling Albert back in the flash once more and being unmercifully beaten by a man thirty pounds lighter and inches smaller than him!"

Just then the fair Albert comes limpin' over to Potts. He looked like he'd been battlin' a buzz saw!

"Mr. Potts," he says, "if you dare to use that scene in your picture, I will bring suit against your firm. I demand that the film be destroyed at once!"

"What you say!" screams Genaro. "Nevaire! She'sa mine, that picture! Away wit' you—you bigga bunk!" He stands before the camera like he's ready and willin' to protect it with his life.

"You entered the scene of your own accord, *Mr. LaRue*," remarks Potts, "and I trust you are in earnest about suing us. The publicity will just about save me a hundred thousand in advertising."

As soon as he heard that name "LaRue," this guy just kinda caves in and closes up tight. Miss Vincent turns her nose up at him and walks over to the Kid as the other dame comes up and shakes Scanlan's hand.

"Thank you!" she says, in that tired voice of hers. "You have done a big thing for me! Now he cannot go into the pictures again, and maybe he'll—he'll stay home with me!"

At that Miss Vincent suddenly leans over and kisses her. Can you beat them dames?

Albert picks up his hat and straightens his tie. Then he glares from one to the other of us and walks over to Genaro.

"I trust," he says, throwin' out his chest. "I trust you realize that if your picture is a success, I, and I alone, am responsible for it. If it hadn't been for the advent of myself, a finished artist, in that fight scene, it would have fallen flat! Good day, sir!"

And him and his dame and the white-faced Sweet Williams blows!

CHAPTER IV
LEND ME YOUR EARS

I don't mind a four-flusher if his stuff is good, know what I mean? A guy that makes the world think he's there forty ways when as a matter of fact, he's *shy* about sixty, deserves credit. Usually, them birds get it too! They know more about credit than the guy that wrote it, and any butcher, grocer, tailor or the like who figures on 'em settlin' the old account has no right to be in business. The only time a four-flusher pays off is when he hits a new town. Then, if the attendance is good, he'll buy four or five evenin' papers right out loud in front of everybody, carelessly displayin' a couple of yellow bills that might be fifties —if they wasn't tens. After that outburst, all he spends is the week end.

For the benefit of them which live in towns where the total vote for President sounds like the score of a world series game, I'll explain what a four-flusher is, although they probably got one in their midst, at that. You'll generally find *one* wherever there's two people—men or women. A four-flusher is a guy who claims he can lick Jack Dempsey in a loud and annoyin' voice, and then runs seven blocks in five minutes flat when some hick in the back room arises to remark that he's willin' to take a beatin' for Jack. A four-flusher is the bird that breezes down Main street in a set of scenery that would make John Drew look like one of the boys in the gas main trenches somewheres in Broadway, and yet couldn't purchase an eraser, if rubber was sellin' at three cents a ton. A four-flusher is a hick that admits bein' a better singer than Caruso, a better ball-player than Ty Cobb, a better real estate judge than Columbus and more of a chance taker than Napoleon.

The first time he starts at any one of them things, he's a odds-on favorite for last and finishes ten lengths behind the rest of the field. That's a four-flusher.

A guy can be taught paintin', pinochle, politics and

prohibition, but a first-class four-flusher is *born* that way!

Takin' 'em as a league, I'm about as fond of them guys as a worm is of a fisherman. The only one I ever fell for was J. Harold Cuthbert, and that bird had somethin' that the others didn't—he was different! I thought I had seen 'em all, but this guy crossed me, his stuff was new!

The way I met Harold was almost romantic. He was reclinin' on the ground in a careless manner about ten feet away from the main entrance to Film City, and he looked like the loser in a battle royal where the weapons used had been picked out by a guy who hoped there'd be no survivors. He was gazin' up at what the natives insist is a better grade of sky than anything we got in the East, and he looked like he was tryin' to figure whether they was right or not. About two feet away, lumberman's measure, observin' the wreck and yawning was Francis Xavier Scanlan, known to the trade as Kid Scanlan, welterweight champion of the world and Shantung. I looked around for a director and a camera man, but they was nobody else in sight, so figurin' this couldn't be nothin' more than a dress rehearsal, I stepped over to the Kid.

"Who's your friend?" I asks him, noddin' to the sleepin' beauty.

"I seen Genaro lookin' for you," says the Kid. "I'll bet you been over to Frisco tryin' to nail that dame at the Busy Bee, ain't you?"

"A gambler will never get nowheres," I tells him, "but you're startin' off with a win on that bet!" I points at the model for still life again. "When does that guy get up?" I inquires.

The Kid looks down at him for a minute, proddin' him carelessly with his foot.

"Weather permittin'," he answers, "he ought to be on his feet in five more minutes, and I'd never have raised a finger to him, if he hadn't come at me first!"

"D'ye mean to say you been wallopin' that guy?" I says.

"Well, what does it look like?" sneers the Kid. "A man's got a right to protect himself, ain't he?"

"He hit you, eh?" I says.

"No!" answers the Kid. "He didn't get that far with it, but he claimed he was goin' to, and naturally it was up to me to stop him from gettin' in a brawl. I never seen a gamer guy in my life, either," he goes on, admirin'ly. "He knows he'll catch cold layin' on the ground like that, and yet the minute I stung him he takes a dive and stays down!"

By this time our hero has risen to his feet and, while dustin' off his clothes, he looks like he's figurin' whether he ought to claim he'd been doped and ask for a return bout, or call it a day and let it go at that. Except for where the Kid had jabbed him, he wasn't a bad lookin' bird, his best bets bein' a crop of dark, wavy hair and a set of features which any movie leadin' man could give ten thousand bucks for and make it up on the first picture. The suit of clothes he was wearin' had probably put the tailor over, and he also had two yellow gloves and a little trick cane. He walks over to where me and the Kid was standin' and takes off his hat. It was one of them dashin', devilish soft things that has names like Pullman cars—you know, "The Bryn Mawr, $2.50. All Harvard Wears One." Then he points at the Kid with his cane.

"I made a serious error," he remarks, "in engaging in a brawl with a thug! I thought you would meet me with a gentleman's weapons and—"

"I ain't got a marshmallow on me," butts in the Kid, grinnin', "or I would have done that thing. You come at me without no warnin', didn't you?"

"Merciful Heaven, what grammar!" says the other guy. "I didn't come at you, as you say in that quaint English of yours, I thought you could take a joke or—"

"Yeh?" interrupts the Kid. "That's what the formerly Kaiser has been tryin' to tell the world, but it ain't goin' into hysterics over his comedy!"

"Well," says the other guy, buttonin' up his coat and glarin' at us both, "this is not the end of the incident, you can rest assured of that! The next time we meet I think the result will be different!"

"Say!" pipes the Kid. "What d'ye think I'm gonna do—fight a world series with you? If you wanna scrap, I know where you can get all the action you can handle."

"And where is that, pray?" asks the other guy.

"Russia!" says the Kid. "You must have seen it in the papers." He pats him on the shoulder. "And now, good-by and good luck," he goes on. "I'm sorry I had to bounce you, but—"

"Enough of this nonsense!" cuts in the other guy, pullin' out a card and passin' it over to the Kid. "My seconds will wait upon you to-morrow. I choose rapiers!"

"You which?" says the Kid, examinin' the card. "I don't make you."

"I said that my choice of weapons is rapiers!" explains this guy. "And as a matter of fairness I must tell you that I have never met my equal with a sword!"

"Are you tryin' to kid me?" asks Scanlan. "What d'ye mean rapiers?"

"Is it possible you have never handled a blade?" exclaims the other guy, like he couldn't have heard it right.

"I used to, at that," admits the Kid, "but now I use a fork, except to pat down the potatoes!"

"So much the worse for you, then!" frowns the sword-swallower. "But you brought it upon yourself. Remember, to-morrow! And—" he stoops over and hisses, "—rapiers, without buttons!"

"Ha, ha!" yells the Kid. "Raypeers without buttons! How are you gonna hold 'em up?"

"Your ignorance is pathetic—not funny!" answers the other guy.

"I know," says the Kid. "I barely got through Yale!" He lays his arm on this guy's shoulder. "Are you on the level with this fight thing?" he asks him.

"I was never more in earnest in my life!" says the knife-thrower.

"Or nearer Heaven!" grins the Kid. "All right!" he goes on. "I'm game, if you are, only there's just one question I'd like to ask before the slaughter begins; don't *I* get no say about the tools we're gonna use?"

This guy thinks for a minute and then nods his head.

"Very well!" he says. "I'll make the concession—an unheard-of thing in the code. What is your choice?"

"Pinochle!" yells the Kid. "I'll stake you to a hundred aces and beat you from here to Denver!"

"Ugh!" snorts the other guy—and castin' a sneer at both of us, he passes in the gate.

We went in after him, and the Kid tells me how he come to flatten this baby, which, from the card he give us, was J. Harold Cuthbert. The Kid says Harold stopped him outside the portals of Film City and asked him why no auto had met him at the train. Scanlan says he didn't know, but he had seen the mayor and two brass bands goin' down and hadn't Harold met 'em? Harold says he had not and he was gonna file a complaint about it, because he was the greatest movie actor that ever bawled out a director. With that, says the Kid, he reeled off the names of the pictures he had been featured in, and from the list he give out the only thing he wasn't featured in was "Microbes at Play," a educational film tore off by the company last year. The Kid asks him if he ever heard of Kid Scanlan, the shop girls' delight, who was bein' starred in a five-reeler called "Lay Off, MacDuff." Harold throwed out his chest and says he wrote it and practically made Scanlan by directin' it. At that the Kid tells him that he may be a movie star, but he looks like a liar to him. Harold makes a pass at him, and Scanlan hit him to see would he bounce.

He didn't, and he was just comin' around when I blowed on the scene.

When we got to Genaro's office, Harold was tellin' Eddie Duke the reason he was bunged up was because he had fell off the train comin' out, and Eddie says that was tough and it was time Congress got after them railroads, but the thing he'd like to know was why Harold had come out at all. They had looked up the files and there was nothin' to show who had ordered this guy shipped on.

Harold looks over the bunch in the office for a minute, registers "I-am-thinking-deeply," and then snaps his fingers.

"Oh!" he says. "I had a letter of introduction from Mr. Potts, but I suppose it's in my gray morning suit which will arrive with my trunks in a day or so. Mr. Potts and myself are old friends," he winks at Genaro confidentially. "I really think my father owns a slew of the company's stock, but then Dad is connected with so many vast enterprises that—"

"Joosta wan minoote!" interrupts Genaro, turnin' a cold eye on Harold. "Joosta wan minoote! We're very busy joosta now, sometime nex' week everybody she'sa listen about your father. What we wanna know is what Meester Potts he'sa senda you out here to do?"

"Yeh!" says Duke. "That's the idea—what's your act?"

"Why, I intend to play romantic leads," pipes Harold, "and I have an idea that—"

"Ha, ha!" laughs the Kid. "That's fair enough. All Edison had was a idea, and look at him now!"

Harold frowns at him and walks over to Miss Vincent.

"How do you do, Miss Vincent," he says, takin' off his hat and presentin' her with a bow. "I knew you at once from your photographs. I have a remarkable memory, inherited from my father. The late J. P. Morgan once said of him, during the course of a gigantic stock deal, that—but enough of personalities. I saw you in the 'Escapades of Eva.'"

"Did you like me?" smiles Miss Vincent.

"Very much!" Harold tells her. "Although the mediocre support and execrable direction spoiled most of your opportunities. Now if *I* had directed that picture, you would have been a great deal—"

"Joosta wan minoote!" butts in Genaro, gettin' red in the face. "I, Genaro, directed that picture!"

Harold looks over at him and lights a cigarette.

"Well," he says, flickin' the ash in Genaro's drinkin' glass, "I daresay you did your best! But had *I* been there when the picture was being produced, I would have suggested a great many things that would have greatly improved it. I remember calling Belasco's attention to a detail one time and Dave said to me—"

"Enough!" snaps Genaro, glarin' at him. "You will report to Meester Duke. He'sa tella you what to do. Or maybe," he snorts, "maybe *you* tella heem!"

And he stamps out of the office.

"What a quaint little man!" says Harold, sittin' down in Genaro's chair and glancin' with interest over some letters that was on his desk. "How do those chaps ever get into the movies?"

"Ow!" whispers Duke. "If the quaint little man had only heard that!" He turns, to Harold. "I don't know where I can place you right away," he says. "How are you on Shakespeare? We're putting on a seven reeler of 'As You Like It' with Betty Vincent as Rosalind. Do you think you could do Orlando?"

Harold throws out his chest and sneers.

"What a question!" he remarks. "I could eat it up!"

"I don't want you to eat it," says Duke, gettin' sore. "If you can play it, I'll be satisfied! You had better go over and register at the hotel now, and, when you come back, we'll go over the thing."

Harold gets up, yawns and looks at Miss Vincent.

"I'll show you an entirely new interpretation of Rosalind, Miss Vincent," he tells her. "Of course, Shakespeare was clever after a fashion, but *I*—however," he breaks off and holds out his arm. "Would you care to walk about the grounds here a bit, so that I may illustrate some of the salient points in my version?"

"No!" cuts in the Kid, before she can answer. "On your

way!" he says. "Miss Vincent's got a date with me to find out is it true you can make ninety miles an hour in a 1921 Automatic!"

"But—but, my dear sir—" splutters Harold. "I—you—"

"Listen, Stupid," says the Kid. "I can't be bouncin' you all day, but if you don't canter along, I'll make you hard to catch!"

Miss Vincent smiles and grabs the Kid by the arm.

"Let us have no violence!" she says. "You can tell me all about Rosalind when I return, Mr. Cuthbert."

"Yeh," adds the Kid. "I'll be willin' to stand for a earful of it myself, then."

And they breeze out of the office.

"Heavens, what an uncouth ruffian!" pipes Harold, lookin' after 'em. "I wonder Miss Vincent trusts herself in his company."

"She's a whole lot safer with him than you'd be, old top!" I says. "And if I was you, I'd lay off that uncouth ruffian stuff around the Kid. Don't keep temptin' him, because he's liable to get sore, and when Scanlan gets mad you want to be in the next county!"

"Huh!" sneers Harold. "What does he do, pray?"

"Well," I says, "I'll tell you. I don't get that dewpray thing of yours, but the last time the Kid got peeved he won the welterweight title! Is that good enough?"

"He had better look to his laurels," remarks Harold, "for if he insults me again, he'll lose them! I'm rather a master of boxing, and at home I won several medals as an amateur heavy —"

"I suppose," I butts in, "I suppose you left them medals in one of them gray mornin' suits of yours, eh? You didn't have 'em on when the Kid flattened you, did you?"

"I am not fond of vulgar display," he says, "or—"

"What are you wearin' that black eye for then?" I asks him.

He didn't have none ready for that, and I blew.

Well, Harold run true to form.

The next afternoon I seen Duke standin' near the African Desert. He was callin' upon Heaven in a voice that could be heard plainly in Cape May, N. J., to ask it if it had ever seen a actor like J. Harold Cuthbert. Not gettin' no answer, he turned his attention to the other place, and when he seen me he put it up to me.

"What's the matter with Harold?" I asks him. "I thought he was gonna be a knockout in this Shakespeare stuff."

"He was!" says Duke. "The camera men are laughin' yet! Alongside of that big four-flusher, Kid Scanlan would look like Richard Mansfield!"

"He's rotten, eh?" I says.

"Rotten?" yells Duke. "Why, say—callin' him *rotten* is givin' him a *boost*! If that big stiff is an actor, I'm mayor of Shantung! He don't know if grease paint is to put on your face or to seal letters with, he's got the same faculty of expression on that soft putty map of his as an ox has, he makes love like a wax dummy and he come out to play 'As You Like It' in a dress suit! It took eight supers to keep him away from in front of the camera, and he played one scene with his face glued up against the lens!"

Just then Harold himself eases into view with the Kid taggin' along at his side. Scanlan is excited about somethin' and wavin' his arms, but Harold still has that old sneer on his face, and as they come up, I hear him sayin' this,

"My dear fellow, I know more about auction pinochle than Hoyle. At home I am recognized as the champion card player of—" He breaks off, when he sees us, and turns to Duke. "Hello!" he calls over. "Are you ready to admit now that my idea of making feature productions is the right one?"

"No!" snarls Duke. "But I'll concede that as an actor you're a crackerjack bartender! D'ye mean to tell me that you got away with that kind of stuff in the studios back East?"

"I introduced it!" says Harold, proudly. "As a director for some of the largest film companies in the world, I have put on hundreds of—"

"The only thing you ever put on was your hat!" interrupts Duke. "And I bet that give you trouble on account of the size of your head. I suppose you're gonna tell me that you're also a scenario writer, a camera man and the guy that got Nero's permission to film the burnin' of Rome, eh?"

"The last is something of an exaggeration," pipes Harold, "but as far as the other things you mentioned are concerned, I must confess that there are few people in the business who have approached me!"

"Ain't that rich?" whispers the Kid to me. "You got to hand it to this bird!"

"You'd be a wonder as a press agent!" I says to Harold.

"Now that's odd you should remark that," he smiles. "For, as a matter of fact, I excel in *that* field! I did all the press work for—"

"Columbus!" yells Duke, wavin' him off. "Good-by!" he goes on. "I got enough! You got a liar lookin' like George Washington!"

Harold looks after Duke as he went into the office.

"Heavens!" he says. "I can't stand that man with his petty little jealousies! Now when I—"

I don't know what the rest of it was, because me and the Kid left him to tell it to the African Desert.

Well, Genaro bein' afraid to get in dutch with Potts, which accordin' to Harold was a ex-roommate of his, give this guy a crack at everything from directin' to supin', and Harold hit .000 at 'em all. The only thing he seemed to be any good at was talkin' about himself, and he was champion of the world at that! He was willin' to concede that Wellington beat Napoleon and it was Fulton who doped out the steamboat, but *he* was the guy that had put over everything else. His favorite word only had one letter in it, and that's the one that comes right after H. No matter what subject would come up anywheres where Harold could get a earful of it, he was the bird that invented it!

We went down to Montana Joe's one afternoon to deal prohibition a blow, and the Kid gets talkin' about drinkin' as a art, carelessly lettin' fall the information that, before he had put the Demon Rum down for the count, he had been looked on as a champion at goin' through the rye. He winks at Joe and orders a tumbler of private stock. Harold never bats a eye, but says he's got a roomful of lovin' cups which was give him for emptyin' bottles. Joe sets down a mixin' glass full of booze before the Kid, and Scanlan looks at Harold and asks Joe what was the matter with the shaker. Harold coughs and raps on the bar. "You may let me have a seidel of gin!" he says, sneerin' at the Kid—and we all fainted!

He got run out the south gate one afternoon by a enraged scene painter for tellin' the latter that he could shut both eyes, bind one arm, lay flat on his side and paint a better exterior than the two hundred dollar a week decorator, and he started a riot in the developin' room another time by remarkin' that the bunch in there didn't know how to paste up film—adding of course, that *he* did. He tried to show Van Aylstyne how to write scenarios, and Van Aylstyne threatened to quit cold if Harold wasn't called off, and when he found fault with Genaro's lightin' of a night scene, Genaro chased him all over the place with a practical shotgun.

It wouldn't have been so bad, if Harold had come through on *somethin'*. If he had discovered *anything*, he could actually do even half way decent, he would have got away with murder. But no!—That bird was the original No Good Nathan, from Useless, Miss.

The fact that he didn't cause no sensation in our midst, worried Harold about as much as the price of electric fans keeps 'em awake in Iceland. There was only one thing Harold was afraid of—and that was lockjaw!

Then Potts blows in unexpected one afternoon, and we all stood around to see him and Harold fall on each other's neck. In fact, pretty near everybody in Film City watched the reunion which took place on the edge of the Street Scene in Tokio—it was very affectin'.

Potts comes walkin' along with three supers and Eddie Duke carryin' his suitcases, when Harold bumps into the parade at the corner. Genaro had sent him over to Frisco for a lot of props that would be needed in a picture he was puttin' on, and naturally, now that Potts was on hand, he was anxious to have everything O.K. He had give Harold a list in the mornin' that read like a inventory of a machine shop, and here's friend Harold comin' back with nothin' in his hands but his fingers.

"The props—where are they?" shrieks Genaro. "Seven hour you have been gone and you come back with nothing! Everything she'sa ready and we musta wait till you come with the props—where are they—queek?"

"My dear fellow," says Harold, bowin' to Miss Vincent, "there is no excuse for addressing me before these ladies and gentlemen in that ruffianly manner. I was unable to carry out your—er—orders this morning, having overlooked a trifling detail in the scurry and bustle of catching that ungodly early train."

"What!" screams Genaro, doin' a few cabaret steps. "You got nothing? *Sapristi*! What you do—make fun of me? Why you no get those props?"

"Calm yourself!" pipes Harold. "I'll tell all. I forgot the list of articles you gave me and—"

"Aha—he'sa maka me crazee!" yelps Genaro, pullin' a swell clog step. "Take heem away before I keel heem!"

Just then Potts comes by, and we all yell, "Welcome to Film City, Mr. Potts!" Harold hears this and turns pale. He seen we was all watchin' closely for the grand reunion between him and his old college chum Potts. He coughs a couple of times and takes a step forward. That boy was game!

"How do you do, Mr. Potts?" he says. "Did you—er—have a pleasant trip?"

"Yes," answers Potts, lookin' at him kinda puzzled. "What is your name again? I don't seem to recall it!"

And the boss was supposed to be Harold's dear old college chum!

"Why—er—why—ha! ha!" pipes Harold, dyin' game. "That's odd! Surely you recall—eh—Cuthbert, my name is, you must remember—eh—why in New York we—eh—"

He's about eighty feet up in the air and still soaring with the whole bunch watchin' him and enjoyin' the thing out loud. Potts is lookin' him over like he's a strange fish or somethin'.

"I think you're mistaken!" pipes the boss, cuttin' in on Harold, "I never saw you before in my life!"

With that he passes on, leavin' Harold flat and with no more friends than China had at the Peace Conference.

After that little incident, it was about as pleasant for Harold in Film City as it was for a German in Liverpool durin' the war. Genaro, Duke and everybody else went out of their way to make him sick of the movies, but Harold stuck around and took whatever odd jobs that come his way with the remark that he could do it better than anybody else and that was why they give it to him.

I made a mistake when I said everybody rode him—he had three little pals. They was Miss Vincent, the Kid and yours in the faith. Miss Vincent claimed that after all he was only a boy which would grow out of lyin', if give enough time, and it was a outrage the way everybody picked on him. The Kid said we couldn't all be perfect, and Miss Vincent would give him back his presents if he laid off Harold. *My* excuse for not shootin' Harold was that I liked one thing about him, and that was the way he hung on, no matter how they was breakin' for him. He was no good all over, but he wouldn't *quit* and any guy that could stand up under punishment like he did is worth a cheer any time—and sometimes a bet!

I thought I'd brighten his life by tellin' him how he stood with the three of us. I pictured him goin' down on his knees and thankin' me with tears in his eyes, when I said that we was with him to the bitter end. He must have had rheumatism or a pair of charley horses, because he failed to do any kneelin' where I could see it, and his eyes was as dry as the middle of Maine. Instead of that, he took me for ten bucks and said the news was no surprise to him. He didn't see how Miss Vincent could miss likin' him, because he had been a assassin with the women from birth. As for the Kid, well, it was common talk that Scanlan was afraid of him, and I was nothin' but a sure-thing player which knowed he was a winner and stuck, hopin' I'd cash.

Could you tie Harold?

Van Aylstyne, the guy that committed the scenarios, went out one night to get some atmosphere for a thriller at Montana Joe's. He got the atmosphere O.K., bringin' most of it back on his breath and the Kid asked him to stick out his tongue so he could see was they any revenue stamps on it. In the mornin' he grabbed a container of ice water and a pen and dashed off a atrocity in five reels based on what atmosphere of Montana Joe's that was still with him. He called the thing "The End of the World!" Potts says the title alone sounded good enough to him to remove the bumpers from his bankroll without lookin' further, addin', in a loud aside, that if the plot wasn't a knockout, Van Aylstyne could change the title to "The End of My Job!" De Vronde, the popular heart-breaker, is given the lead opposite Miss Vincent, and, of course, Kid Scanlan is to be dragged in as a special feature. Harold has hypnotised Genaro into lettin' him take off a "enter with others" in the first reel. Everything was ready to have the cameras pointed at it, when somethin' come along that balled it all up.

Her name was Gladys O'Hara.

Gladys was no ravin' beauty and I heard her say "ain't it" twice, but she was one of them dames that the first flash you get at 'em you wonder are they still enforcin' the law against mashers! She had a wonderful complexion and although if you looked close you could see she had give nature a helpin' hand, she did the retouchin' so well that you was glad she had. She had one of the latest model, twin-six figures and she dressed with the idea of givin' the natives a treat, even if she was takin' chances on pneumonia. Gladys was the kind of dame that starts the arguments in the newspapers on what is our offices comin' to, look how them stenographers dress!

When J. Harold Cuthbert met Gladys, she had got as far as bein' a saleslady in the Busy Bee, Frisco. She could have beat that with her eyes closed, but Gladys kept hers open and, bein' a female wise guy, she knew who to eat lunch with and who to say, "I don't get you!" to—which is a art! As a result, she had never got no further than sellin' shirtwaists and had her first home to break up. She never advanced beyond that counter—up or down! Many a necktie salesman had flashed Gladys and gone right out to buy the tickets, before he even asked her would she look over a show, windin' up by throwin' 'em away and tellin' her what a sweet old woman his mother was and how strong he was for his own gas meter. That was Gladys. She looked like what she wasn't, and she fooled 'em all.

All but Harold!

I found Gladys very easy to look at myself, and I helped the Sante Fe over a tough year by runnin' over to Frisco to the Busy Bee whenever I could get away. It took me a short month to find out that I had the same chance of winnin' out as I'd have of gettin' elected King of Montenegro by acclamation, because Harold had been there first and got in his deadly work.

I was standin' in the next aisle to where Gladys held

forth, one afternoon, waitin' for a couple of fatheads to call it a day and move away from the counter, when along comes Harold. As usual, he was all dressed up like a horse, with the even fare back to Film City in them one-way pockets of his. He butts right into the conversation, and I nearly fainted when he passes a box of candy over to Gladys. Then I seen the label on the package, and I revived, because it was one of a dozen that some simp had sent Miss Vincent and in order to please the Kid she had give 'em all away. Harold had brought his all the way over to Frisco on a ticket furnished by the Maudlin Movin' Picture Company, which sent him over for props.

Well, Harold gets warmed up and in a minute he's press agentin' himself at the rate of fifty-five words a minute—I clocked him! He tells Gladys he's bein' *starred* in "The End of the World" and the amount of money they're payin' him would startle Europe, if it ever got out. He claims he made 'em all faint at the rehearsals and offers from other companies is comin' in so fast that he's got a charley horse on his thumb from openin' telegrams. From that he works into the fact that after the picture is made he's gonna run around Europe—that's just the way he said it, "Run around Europe!" Oh, boy!—that bein' the way he usually spent his vacations. When Gladys staggers over to wait on a customer, Harold charges himself up again and when she comes back he's off to a runnin' start. He remarks that his father has just made a killin' in Wall Street that has caused Rockefeller to weep and gnash his teeth and that the last affair his mother give at Newport got four columns on the front page, although the mayor of the town had been shot the same afternoon.

Gladys takes this all in with her mouth as open as Kelly pool and her eyes half closed and dreamy like she was dyin' happy.

When Harold put on the brakes and eased up, she threw him a look that I would have walloped Dempsey for. Harold says he must go, because the picture would be ruined if he wasn't there to direct it, and Gladys holds out a tremblin' hand. Then Harold plays his ace—he takes off his hat, bows, kisses that hand and blows.

When I seen Gladys deliberately walk back of the wrappin' booth, put her hand to her lips and kiss it herself—I pulled my hat down over my ears and went back to Film City.

The next mornin' they begin work on the first reel of "The End of the World," and Harold had a field day at bein' rotten. He got in everybody's way, ruined twenty feet of film by firin' off a cannon at the wrong time and made Genaro hysterical by gettin' caught in a papier mache tower and pullin' it down. Not content with that, he goes back of a interior to try out one of the Kid's cigarettes and by simply flickin' the thing into a can of kerosene he set the Maudlin Movin' Picture Company back about five hundred bucks.

They run him out of the picture, and he went, yellin' that it would be a farce without him in it.

About four o'clock me and the Kid is trottin' along the road outside of Film City like we did every day so's Scanlan could keep in condition, when we all but fell over Harold. He's sittin' on a rock and gazin' off very sad in the general direction of New York. His dashin', smashin', soft hat was yanked down over his home-breakin' face, and his dimpled chin was buried in his lily white hands. He looked like a guy that has worked twenty-seven years inventin' a new steamboat and then seen it sink the first time he tried it out.

The Kid runs over and slaps him on the back just hard enough to make his hat fall off.

"Cheer up, Cutey!" pipes Scanlan. "They can't hang a guy for tryin'!"

Harold retrieves his hat, smoothes it out carefully and lets loose the gloomiest sigh I ever heard in my life.

"Have you a cigarette?" he asks sadly.

The Kid pulls out a deck, and Harold takes two, droppin'

one in his pocket.

"Alas!" he remarks, strikin' a match on my shoe. "Alas!"

"When can the body be seen?" asks Scanlan. "And is it a church funeral or will they pull it off at the house?"

"This is no time for levity," mutters Harold. "I'm ruined!"

"I only got ten bucks with me," the Kid tells him, "but I'll part with—"

"Poof!" sneers Harold, wavin' his hands like a head waiter. "Money! I am not in need of that. Why, my father—" He breaks off to take the bill from the Kid's hand and shove it in his pocket. "Rather than offend you!" he explains. "No," he goes on, "this is a more serious matter than money. I—" He flicks away the cigarette, jumps up off the rock and gives us both the up and down. "I am going to take you two into my confidence," he says, "and perhaps you will help me."

"Go on!" encourages the Kid. "I'm all worked up—shoot it!"

"Well, then," says Harold, with the air of a guy pleadin' guilty to save his old father. "In the first place, my name is not J. Harold Cuthbert!"

There was no answer from us, and Harold seemed peeved because we had not collapsed at his confession.

"What is it?" I asks, when the silence begin to hurt the ears.

"Trout!" pipes Harold, bitterly. "Joe Trout!"

"Yeh?" says the Kid. "Well, what's the matter with that? What did you can it for?"

"Ha, ha!" hisses Harold, with a "curse you!" giggle. "Where could a man get with a name like *that*?"

"In the aquarium!" yells the Kid. "I knew you'd fall!"

Harold shakes his head and blows himself to another sigh.

"Imagine a moving picture leading man named Trout!" he goes on. "I changed my name as a sacrifice to the movies, for—"

"Just a minute!" I butts in. "On the level now, where *did* you get your movin' picture experience?"

"As assistant bookkeeper in a grocery store!" he answers. "Now you have it!"

"But you said your father was a big man in Wall Street!" I busts out.

"He is!" answers Harold, lookin' over at the Santa Fe. "They don't come any bigger. He's a traffic policeman at the corner of Broadway and Wall Street and stands six foot four in his socks!"

"Sweet Cookie!" shouts the Kid, and falls off the rock.

When we recover from that, Harold has smoked the other cigarette, and he nods for my box. Then he asks us do we want to hear the rest.

"If you don't tell it," says the Kid, "you'll never leave here alive! Hurry up, I'm dyin' to hear it!"

"Well," says the ex-J. Harold Cuthbert, "I am about to be married and at the eleventh hour Nemesis has gripped me. I told my fiancée that I was being featured in 'The End of the World' and that it would be exceedingly easy for me to get *her* a part in the picture—she having expressed a desire to that effect at various times. She will be here within the hour to watch me being filmed and to hold me to my promise to place her as leading woman opposite me." He stops and moans. "Gentlemen," he goes on, "picture for yourself the contretemps when she finds I am nothing but a super and that Genaro wouldn't give Sarah Bernhardt a job on a recommendation from me! My romance will be shattered, and the—the humiliation will kill me!"

There was a heavy silence for a minute, and then the Kid whistles.

"Well, pal," he says, "you have certainly balled things up a few, haven't you?"

Joe Trout just let loose another moan.

"Gimme one of them good cigarettes!" pipes the Kid to me. He lights it and looks over at friend Joe. "The first thing," he says, puffin' away; "the first thing, is this—just how *much* do you think of this dame, all jokes aside?"

Joe turns around and straightens up, for once in his life lookin' like the real thing.

"I love her!" he says. That was all—but the way he pulled it was a plenty!

The Kid grunts and tosses away the pill. Then he walks over to Joe and slaps him on the back.

"Listen!" he says. "You ain't a bad guy at that. I'm gonna give you somethin' I never took in my life—advice! Why don't you lay off lyin' about yourself, kid? Why don't you can that four-flush thing?"

The effect of them simple words on Joe was remarkable. He swung around on us so quick that we both ducked, thinkin' he was comin' back with a wallop—but his hands was sunk so deep in his coat pockets they liked to pushed through the linin' and his face was as hard and white as an iceberg.

"Because!" he shoots out through his teeth. "*Because I can't!*"

Y'know the change was so sudden, I remember lettin' out a little nervous laugh, and then sidesteppin' a vicious left the Kid sent at me. Scanlan had turned as serious as the other guy.

"What d'ye mean, you *can't*?" he says, grabbin' Joe by the arm and holdin' him fast. Joe's face showed how hard he was fightin' to keep from fallin' apart.

"You won't understand!" he answers in a hard voice. "But I'll tell you. The thing has grown upon me until I cannot shake it off! I guess I was born a liar and probably four-flushed my nurse when I was three days old. When I was a boy, my incessant lying, although it harmed no one but myself, kept me in countless scrapes. As I grew older, the habit grew stronger and I lost girls, jobs, friends and opportunities with breath-taking rapidity. Time after time I have sworn to rid myself of the thing and speak nothing but the undiluted truth, and the first time I open my mouth I find myself unconsciously telling the most astounding falsehoods about myself with an ease that nauseates me!" He tore himself loose from the Kid and kicked a innocent tomato can down the canyon. "I know I'm nothing but a big four-flusher," he winds up, "and I can't help it!"

Right then and there I warmed up to Joe Trout like I never had before. After all, Miss Vincent had the right dope—he was nothin' but a big kid at that, and any guy that will come right out in public and admit he's a false alarm, deserves credit!

"Well," he says after a minute, "I suppose you're both through with me now, eh?"

"Do I look like a quitter?" demands the Kid.

"I'm still here, ain't I?" I chimes in.

Joe coughs and took hold of our hands.

"Thanks!" he mutters. "And now—-"

"Listen!" interrupts the Kid. "I got the whole thing doped out. When is this dame of yours due to hit Film City?"

"She'll be here on that one o'clock train," moans Joe.

"Fine!" says the Kid. "Now get this! De Vronde is supposed to do a fall from a horse in 'The End of the World' and the big yellow bum won't do it. They're lookin' for some guy that will take his place, just for that one flash, see? Now suppose I fix it so you get that chance and when the dame comes on, there you are playin' the lead as far as she can see, in the best part of the frolic. How's that?"

I thought Joe was gonna kiss him!

"I'll never forget it!" he hollers. "You have saved my life! What can I do to repay you?"

"Stop four-flushing," comes back the Kid, "and be on the level!"

"I'll do it, if it kills me!" promises Joe—and I don't know whether he meant the fall or the other.

"Can you ride a horse?" the Kid asks him as we start back.

"Can *I* ride a horse?" repeats Joe, stoppin' short. "What a question! Why at home I was the champion—"

"Now, now!" butts in the Kid. "There you go again!"

"Pardon me!" says Joe, gettin' red—and he quits!

Well, the Kid fixed it all right, so's Joe could double for De Vronde in that one place where he did the fall. I don't know how he did it any more than I know how Edison come to think of the phonograph, but he did! All my suspicions as to who the dame was come true when Gladys hops off the one o'clock train that afternoon. I seen her talkin' to Eddie Duke near the African Desert, and I immediately went scoutin' around for Joe, because Eddie liked him the same way the brewers is infatuated with the Anti-Saloon League and I knowed if Eddie got a chance to harpoon Joe with Gladys, he'd do that thing.

About half a hour later, Genaro asks me to go over and find Potts, because they're ready to start shootin' the picture and when I got near the hotel I seen a couple of people blockin' the little narrow passage in back of it. They was Gladys O'Hara and Joe Trout and when I got close up I heard Joseph talkin'. He was goin' like a house on fire and his little old lyin' apparatus was hittin' on all cylinders and runnin' smooth without a break. He explains to Gladys that he went on only in the important part of the picture which she would see in a minute, and that De Vronde was only one of the cheap help who played the part while *he* was restin' for the big scene. As soon as that come up—and he said the whole picture was built around it—they give De Vronde the gate and in went the darin' Joe.

He was all dressed up in a Stetson hat, a cute little yellow silk handkerchief twisted around his manly neck and more chaps than any cow puncher ever wore on his legs outside of a movie. He looked like what he'd liked to have been.

"—and not only that," he winds up, "but they are going

to feature my name on all the advertising for the picture!"

"Is that all?" asks Gladys in a queer little voice.

Joe looked surprised. I guess it was the first time anybody had asked for more!

"Well—no!" he starts off again briskly. "Of course, I am —"

"Wait!" says Gladys, grabbin' his arm. "Don't tell me any more lies! They are not featuring you in this or any other picture! You are not the leading man, you are only a super! Your father is not a millionaire and you cannot get me a job with the Maudlin Moving Picture Company! You're simply a big four-flusher and that lets you out!"

Say! On the level, I thought Joe was gonna pass away on his feet! If I was give to faintin', I'd have been stretched out cold, myself. He got white and then he got red, then he got white again and red again for fully a minute. He tried eighteen times by actual count to say something but that well known tongue of his had laid down at last and quit! He couldn't even raise a whisper.

"I knew you were four-flushin' the first time you started to hand me that stuff!" goes on Gladys, sweetly. "I happen to know the folks here, includin' the leadin' man, De Vronde. He was hangin' around that shirtwaist counter before you knew whether they made pictures here or sponge cake. Also, some of your friends come over from time to time and tipped me off about you, so that I was all set when you started!"

Joe whirls around on her at that, and although this bird had beat me to the wire with Gladys, I felt sorry for him right then. The poor kid was hangin' on the ropes waitin' for somebody to throw in the sponge.

"If you knew all that," he says, kinda choked, "why—why did you let me come over and continue to—to mislead you?"

Gladys coughs and places three or four stray hairs exactly back of her little white ear, gazin' at her wrist watch like it's the first time she ever seen one, and she's wonderin' can it really go. The big boob stands there lookin' at her and the chance of a couple of lifetimes is slippin' away. What? Say, listen! I don't know much about women—fighters is my line—but there was a look on Gladys's face that I'd seen Genaro work two hours one time to put on Miss Vincent's when they was takin' a big picture. So you can figure she wasn't registerin' hate!

"Well, why?" demands Joe again.

"This stuff is all new to me," says Gladys, with a sigh, "but I guess I've got to do it!" She gazes at the ground and gets kinda red. "It was not your conversation that made the hit with me!" she winds up softly.

"I'm afraid I don't understand," pipes Senseless Joe.

"Heavens!" remarks Gladys. "There's enough concrete between your neck and your hat to build a bridge over the bay! I can safely say you're the first man I ever proposed to, but somebody's got to do it and I guess I'm the goat!"

"What!" screams Joe, comin' to life at last. "You—you—forgive—you—" The poor simp gets all excited and once again he can't talk and—I don't blame him. You never seen Gladys, and you don't know how she looked right then!

"Say!" says Gladys. "Am I bein' kidded or—"

Joe might have been a tramp as a movie lover, but take it from me, as the real thing he was no slouch! I hadda stand there and watch it, because I couldn't get past till they got away and if they'd ever seen me, I guess Joe would have bought a gun. Finally, they break, Gladys pushin' Joe away and holdin' him off.

"You've got to promise me you'll stop lyin' and four-flushin'!" she tells him. "Tell the truth and don't kid yourself that you'd have been President, if you hadn't been jobbed. That stuff is poor and will get you nowheres. Make good and you won't have to tell anybody about it—it'll be in the papers! As far as I can see, the best thing about you right now is ME! If you can't get over with *that*, I'll see that you do!"

"We'll get married to-night!" yelps Joe. "There's a minister in Film City and—"

"Don't crowd me!" interrupts Gladys, lettin' herself be kissed. "Do you promise?"

"Anything!" grins Joe.

"Just what *are* you supposed to do in this picture?" she asks him.

"Fall off a horse!" says Joe.

"Is that all?" asks Gladys.

Joe nods.

"Well," Gladys tells him, "you won't do it! I don't want no crippled bridegroom at my weddin'. Now listen to me! If you could *write* that stuff you've been wastin' on the air around here, you ought to make a pretty good press agent. Mr. Potts, the man who owns the company and the fellow you or your father *never* palled around with, has a man on his payroll named Struther. He's head of what they call the publicity department, it says so on ten of his cards I have. He once claimed he'd do anything for me in such a loud voice that the floorwalker had to speak to him. I'm goin' over to the office now and ask him to give you a job back in New York. To be perfectly truthful with you, that's what I came over here for to-day in the first place!"

"But—but," stammers Joe. "I can't have you asking favors for me, Gladys, and—and, why New York?"

"Because," she says, "that's where I come from, and I want to look at it again—I'm simply crazy to yell down a dumbwaiter and throw a quarter in my own gas meter!"

Well—that's about all. They had a big weddin' right in the middle of Film City and everybody sent in and bought 'em a present. Potts got a flash at Gladys, moans regretfully and has the ceremony filmed, givin' the result to Joe as a special gift. Of course Gladys got Joe that job. That dame could have got frankfurters and sourkraut in Buckingham Palace! Before they left for New York, I tried Joe out.

"It'll be terrible here, when you're gone!" I says, "because you know more about makin' movies than Rockefeller does about oil."

Joe shakes his head and grins.

"No!" he says. "I guess I don't know much about anything!"

I pronounced him cured to myself and shook his hand. The Kid went to the train with him and his bride. I didn't feel up to seein' that guy goin' away with Gladys.

I met the Kid as he was comin' up from the railroad station, and seein' he was laughin', I asked him if the happy pair got off all right.

"Yeh!" he says. "Everything went fine. Me and Miss Vincent waited till the train was pullin' out. Gladys was inside and Joe was standin' on the steps of the Pullman, talkin'. Just before the thing pulled out, I shook Joe's hand and said I hoped he got past in New York, because it was a big burg and a tough one for losers." The Kid stops and laughs some more.

"Well," I says, "what's the joke?"

"Sweet Papa!" says the Kid, wipin' his eyes. "Joe's face lights all up and that old glitter comes back in his eyes!

"'Make good?' he yells to me. 'Well, I ought to make good—my father owns half the town, and I was the biggest thing in it when I left!'"

CHAPTER V.
"EXIT, LAUGHING"

Every time I see one of them big, fat, dignified guys that looks like they have laid somebody eight to five they can go through life without smilin' once, I wonder just how much they'd give in American money to be able to put on a suit of pink pajamas and walk down Fifth Avenue some crowded afternoon, leadin' a green elephant by a string!

I'll bet they's many a bank president, brigadier-general and what not, that would part with their right eye if they could only force themselves to let down for five minutes, can this dignity thing and give a imitation of what a movie comedian thinks is humor. The best proof of this is that the first chance any of them birds gets—*that's just what they do*!

Y'know, you've seen in the papers lots of times where Archibald Van Hesterfeld has been among the starters in the bazaar for the relief of the heat prostration victims in Iceland, or words to that effect. Or, if it wasn't Archibald it might have been General Galumpus or Commodore Fedink—or all of them. Away down at the bottom of the page, if it's a copy of the Succotash Crossing *Bugle*, or right up in the headlines, if it's a big town sheet, after readin' what dignity and so forth the "distinguished guests lent to the affair," you'll see that at midnight they was large doin's on the dance floor. It is even bein' whispered around that the general, commodore or governor fox-trotted with the girls from the Follies and one-stepped with such of the fair sex as cared practically nothin' for the neighbors. Along about the time the milkman was sayin', "Well, here's another day!", the well known distinguished guests was actin' like a guy who knows a Harvard man does, after they have beat Yale or vice versa.

One of them birds acts so dignified at the office all day that not even the most darin' of his clerks would *think* of a joke in the same room with him. He'll breeze home on baby's birthday with a trick lion or a jumpin' jack for the kid, and spend three or four hours on the dinin'-room floor makin' it go, while friend infant wishes to Heaven father would call it a day and commence readin' the papers, so's *he* could toy with it for a while.

The rest of the family stands around and tells each other that the old man must have a good heart at that, because look how he goes out of his way to amuse the baby. Father growls up at 'em and prays that they'll all go to bed, includin' the one that's just learnin' to walk, so's he can be let alone to really enjoy the thing himself!

We're all babies at heart, and the reason most of us don't admit it and give in to our childish desires is because we're afraid the people in the next flat will think we're nutty or have found a way to beat prohibition. Now and then some extry brave guy sneers at the neighbors and lets himself loose, and shortly afterward a committee is appointed to look after his money. Finally, he is shipped f.o.b. to some sanitarium where a passin' nod from the head doctor is listed at twenty-five bucks and where the victim is fed strange foods and tucked in bed at the devilish hour of nine.

This is naturally very discouragin' to the rest of us which was about to tear loose ourselves, so we sigh, growl at the universe—and lay off!

I feel sorry for the guys that have to have their comedy served up to them in disguise, like lobster a la Newburg, for instance. These birds claim they like stuff you got to study for five minutes before you get it, and then at a given signal you pull a nice lady-like laugh, the while remarkin', "How subtle!" You don't want to cackle too loud or the people across the hall will get the idea that you're a tribe of lowbrows, and it'll get said around that your great-grandfather was known to go in hysterics over the funny sheet of the Sunday papers!

They think the vaudeville or movie cut-up that does the

funny falls is a vulgar lunatic who ought to be in jail, and their idea of the height of humor is the way a iceman pronounces décolleté, or somethin' like that.

I like my own comedy straight! I want it to wallop me right on the laugher, so's I can get it the first time and giggle myself sick. I'm extry strong for the loud and common guffaw, and I claim that because I go into hysterics over the fat-man-on-the-banana-peel stuff, it don't prove that I'm a heavy drinker, beat my wife and will probably wind up in jail. On general principles I'm infatuated with the bird that can make me laugh, and I don't care how he does it as long as he makes good. I care not whether he laughs with me or for me, as long as they's a snicker in there somewheres. I can even stand him laughin' at me, because, if his stuff is funny enough—I'll laugh too!

No guy who can look around him, no matter how things is breakin' for him and see somethin' to laugh at as the mob goes by, is beat. That bird is just gettin' ready to pull a new punch from somewheres and he's the baby you want to watch! The guy that can't see nothin' funny in life, whether he's eight or eighty, is through!

Me and Kid Scanlan saved one of them guys. His name was Jason Van Ness.

I was sittin' in Genaro's office one afternoon about seven or eight months after me and the Kid had decided to give the movies a boost, when the door opens and in comes a guy which at first glance I figured must at least be the governor of the state. He's there with a cane, a high hat and the general makeup of a Wall Street broker in a play where he won't forgive his son for marryin' the ingenue. Also, he's built all over like a heavyweight champ, except his face, the same runnin' to the dignified lines of the bloodhounds, them big, flabby, over-lappin' jaws—get me?

"I say, old chap—are you Mister Genaro?" he pipes.

"Nope!" I says. "I'm Johnny Green, manager of Kid Scanlan, welterweight champion of the world."

"Really!" he remarks.

"Well," I says, "d'ye wanna see the contract or will we go over to a notary so's I can swear to it?"

At that he frowns and waves a finger at me.

"Come, my man," he says, "no chaffing now! You may tell Mister Genaro I have arrived! Of course you know who I am?"

That "my man!" thing was a trifle more than I could take! I throws my feet up on Genaro's desk and give this guy a long, careless once over, puttin' everything I had on the stare.

"I ain't got no more idea who you are," I tells him finally, "than a oyster has of roller-skatin'. Who are you? I never seen *your* face on no postage stamps!"

"Oh, I say!" he busts out, registerin' wild indignation. "Don't you ever read the newspapers?"

"Sure!" I says. "But then, escapin' convicts don't get much space in 'em any more! At that, I think I know you now, though."

"I should think you jolly well would!" he comes back, calmin' down some. "Why—"

"Yes!" I goes on. "I got you. I've met so many from your lodge it's funny I didn't recognize the high signs right away. You're a big, tinhorn four-flusher!"

Sweet Cookie!

His face did a Georgie Cohan, gettin' red, white and blue by turns, and he pawed the air, gaspin' for breath like a fat piano mover. Before he can get set for a comeback, they's a loud crash outside the door, followed by the well known dull thud. In another minute Kid Scanlan walks in, draggin' somethin' after him by the back of the neck.

"Look what *I* found!" chirps the Kid, droppin' the thing on the floor.

"By Jove!" squeals the big guy. "He's killed my dresser!"

I got up from the chair and took a flash. Sure enough, the

thing the Kid had dragged in was a human bein'. He was a long, lean guy, lookin' like he'd been over here about long enough to tell the judge that George Washington discovered America, was president now and stopped the Civil War, and can he please have his first papers, so's he can vote against suffrage.

His one good eye opens and examines the room. Then he hops off the floor, shoots a hand inside his pocket and yanks it out with a thing that looked like a undeveloped spear.

"*Sapristi*!" he remarks loudly—and makes a dive at the Kid.

The chair I throwed at him was wasted, because Scanlan stepped aside and flattened the assassin with a left hook to the jaw. The big guy gives one yell and rushes out of the office.

"Who's your friend?" I asks the Kid, pointin' to the sleepin' beauty on the floor.

The Kid glares down at the body and prods it with his foot.

"The big stiff!" he says. "I should have murdered him!"

"Well," I tells him soothin'ly, "it ain't too late yet! What started the mêlée?"

He sits on the side of the desk and lights a cigarette.

"This hick is standin' outside here," he begins, "when I come along as peaceful as the Swiss navy. I see right away he's a Eyetalian, and I'm anxious to show him I can talk his chatter so —"

"Wait a minute!" I butts in. "Since when have *you* been able to speak Eyetalian?"

"What?" he snorts. "Another one, eh? Ain't Miss Vincent been teachin' me English, French, Eyetalian and what to do with the oyster fork?"

"Is she?" I comes back. "That's all new to me. The last flash I got you was just takin' up how to enter a room!"

"Well, I'm past that," he explains, "and next week I begin on manners. Anyhow, I see this boob standin' there, and I says to myself, here's a chance to pull a little Eyetalian. So with that I stands in front of him and says, '*Bomb Germo, Senorita—a vostrican salute!*'"

The Kid stops and bangs his fist down on the table.

"What d'ye think the big hick said?" he asks me.

I passed.

"He grins at me, waggles his shoulders and pipes, '*No spika da Engleesh!*'"

"'What d'ye mean *English*!' I says. 'That ain't English, that's Eyetalian, Stupid! *Bomb Germo Senorita!*'

"'No spika da Engleesh,' he pipes again.

"I grabs him by the shoulder and swing him around.

"'What part of Italy was you born in?' I inquires. 'Hoboken?'

"'No spika da Engleesh!' he grins.

"By this time my goat was runnin' around wild. I grabbed his other shoulder and looked him in the eye.

"'I'll give you one more chance,' I says; 'cut the comedy now and come through or you're gonna have some bad luck. *Bomb Germo Senorita!*'

"'No spika da Engleesh!' he says.

"With that, havin' took all a human bein' could stand, I let him fall!'"

"Just a minute!" I says, as Scanlan starts for the door. "I want to ask you a question about the Eyetalian language, as long as you know so much about it. Just what does *Bomb Germo* mean?"

The Kid stops and scratches his chin.

"To tell you the truth," he admits, "I don't know!"

At that the door opens and in blows Genaro with the big dignified guy and "Bomb Germo" arises from the floor again, rubbin' the back of his head.

"What's a mat?" asks Genaro, lookin' very excited from me to the Kid. "Why you knock him down Meester Van Ness bureau?"

"Dresser!" corrects Van Ness, puttin' a round piece of glass over one eye and glarin' at us.

"'Scuse a me!" pipes Genaro, makin' a bow. "Why you knock him down Meester Van Ness dresser?"

The Kid growls at "Bomb Germo" who hisses back at him like a snake and backs out of range of that left.

"I asked him 'Bomb Germo,'" explains Scanlan, "and he started to kid me!"

"Bomb Germo? Bomb Germo?" repeats Genaro. "What is she that Bomb Germo?"

Scanlan grunts at him in disgust.

"You're a fine Eyetalian, you are!" he snorts. "I'll bet you and that other guy don't know whether spaghetti is a outfielder or a race horse!"

Van Ness removes the one-cylinder eyeglass for a minute and cleans it with his "for display only" handkerchief.

"Maybe," he remarks. "Maybe the fellow means to say 'Buona Juerno!'"

"Oh!" grins Genaro. "Si! He'sa mean 'Good morning!' No?"

"Yes!" says the Kid. "Correct! Step to the head of the class. I told that to Stupid there and he says, 'No spika da Engleesh!'"

"Well," chirps Genaro, pattin' the Kid on the back, "let's all be the friend now, no? What's the use hava the fight?" He turns to Van Ness and takes his hand, "Meester Van Ness," he goes on, "thisa Meester Kid Scanlan. He'sa tougha nut—but nica fel'. He'sa fighting champion of the world. He'sa taka his fista so," he stops and waves his arms around, "everybody she'sa falla down!" He swings around on the Kid. "Meester Kid Scanlan," he pants, "thisa Meester Van Ness. He'sa greata bigga actor. Oh, of the A numbera seven!"

"Yeh?" says the Kid, registerin' "I-should-worry!" and

gazin' over at "Bomb Germo." "Well, that ain't my fault, is it? Who's the other guy?"

"Guy?" says Genaro. "Whata guy?"

"The phoney wop!" pipes the Kid, pointin' to the long, thin bird.

"Oh, heem!" snorts Genaro, snappin' his fingers. "He'sa nobody. Justa what you call the dresser for the granda Meester Van Ness."

"He's got a name, ain't he?" asks the Kid.

"Joosta Tony," answers Genaro.

"Good enough!" comes back Scanlan, walking across the room. "Hey, Tony!" he says. "They tell me you claim to be a Eyetalian."

"That'sa right!" pipes Tony, forgettin' himself and scowlin'.

"Well," goes on the Kid. "*Bomb Germo!*"

"No spika da Engleesh!" frowns Tony, waggling his shoulders.

"You big stiff!" roars the Kid, gettin' red in the face. "You won't speak nothin' when I get done toyin' with that odd face of yours!"

He makes a dive for Tony, but Genaro grabs him.

"Joosta one minoote!" pants Genaro. "It'sa maka me laugh! Ho, ho, I teenk I getta one, two hysterics! Fighting champion of the world, he'sa getta mad at the dresser!"

"By Jove!" pants Van Ness, givin' the Kid the up and down through the trick eyeglass. "By Jove! I told Tony to converse with no one while we were here. What does this—this person mean by buffeting him about? I thought this company was composed of ladies and gentlemen, not stevedores and longshoremen!"

"Don't get gay, Fatty!" yells the Kid, strugglin' with Genaro. "I put bigger actors than *you* to sleep. I gotta left hand that's got morphine lookin' like a alarm clock!"

"Waita, waita!" shrieks Genaro. "We musta all be the friend. Joosta waita when you and Meester Van Ness get better acquainta you'll be joosta like—"

"Germany and England!" butts in the Kid, tearin' himself away. "Come on!" he tells me. "Let's get away from here," he glares at Van Ness and Tony, "before certain parties makes any more cracks! If they do—I'll make 'em look like models for The Dyin' Gladiator!"

"Don'ta minda heem!" whispers Genaro to Van Ness, as we get over to the door. "He'sa fina fel'. He'sa no hurta the *bambino*—what you call ba-bee. Gotta taka bag of the salts with everything he'sa say. Gotta lots temperament!"

"A ruffian, *I* should say!" remarks Van Ness loudly.

"Bigga bunka!" hisses Tony.

"What?" roars the Kid, swingin' around on them.

"Good day, sir!" pipes Van Ness, steppin' back of the desk.

"No spika da Engleesh!" says Tony, steppin' in back of his boss.

I yanked the Kid outside before violence was had by all.

Jason Van Ness stayed at Film City for about two months. Durin' that time he made as many friends as the ex-Kaiser would pick up in Paris. They was two reasons for this, the first bein' that he was the most dignified and solemn guy I ever seen in my life. Stories that would put a victim of lockjaw in hysterics couldn't coax a snicker from that undertaker's face of his which would have made a supreme court justice look like a clown. In fact, if he'd been a judge and I ever come up before him, I would have took one flash at that face and asked him to gimme life and let it go at that! His favorite smokin'-room story was what causes spots on the sun or somethin' equally excitin', and pretty soon they was a standin' offer of a hundred bucks to the first guy that could make Van Ness laugh!

Some of the greatest comedians the movies ever seen laid

awake nights and become famous on stunts they pulled off for
the sole benefit of Van Ness—and all he did was to inquire if
they was crazy or soused!

The second reason that Van Ness was as unpopular as
snow durin' the world's series was because he was the greatest
actor that ever moaned for the star's dressin'-room.

He was brought on to play the lead in one of them early
Roman frolics where the extry people is called "martyrs" and
hurled to the practical lions in the last reel, whilst the emperor
raises his hand for the slaughter to begin, murmurin' "This is the
end of a perfect day!" When Jason Van Ness walked to the
middle of the arena, throwed one end of his cloak over his
shoulder, faced the camera and give himself up to actin'—well,
you forgot all his bad habits and thanked Heaven for lettin' you
live to see him!

That baby was there!

He was stuck up, he had no friends, he wouldn't laugh,
and he had a trick name and carried a dresser, but, Sweet Papa!—
he was *some* actor!

The Kid and me stood watchin' him the first time he
worked, with our eyes and mouths as open as a mobile crap
tourney.

"Ain't he a bear?" asks Eddie Duke, comin' up. "That's
all two-dollar stuff he's pullin' there, bo! Y' don't see actin' like
that every day, eh?"

"Oh, I don't know!" says the Kid, takin' a fresh slant at
Van Ness. "I bet I could give him a battle in Shakespeare, at that!
I was a riot in 'Richard the Third,' wasn't I?"

"Cease!" sneers Duke. "This bird has got them classics
layin' down and rollin' over when he snaps his fingers. Did you
ever see him in 'Quo Vadis'?"

"No!" says the Kid. "But I seen him in tights when they
was—"

Just then Miss Vincent comes along. She's in the picture

with Van Ness, playin' the beautiful Christian martyr which is tied to the lion's back in the fourth reel, because she won't quit chantin' "Now I lay me—" or somethin' like that. After that they throw her to the panthers with Abe Mendelowitz, another Christian martyr and the guy that built the scene. She told me that was the story of the thing, and asked me what I thought of it. Personally, I think them martyrs was a lot of boobs. If I'd have been there, I would have bent the knee before them heathen idols and then done my private prayin' elsewhere. The head martyr might have called me yellah, but no lion would have broke his fast on me!

While I'm thinkin' about this, Miss Vincent reminds me that she's waitin' for my verdict on the thing. The last I heard her say was about bein' tied to that lion.

"Well," I says, "I'll tell you. I think it's pretty soft for the lions myself and—"

"How are you and Stupid gettin' along?" butts in the Kid, pointin' to Van Ness and touchin' Miss Vincent's arm.

She frowns.

"You mustn't call him Stupid!" she says. "Mister Van Ness is an artist and a gentleman—and—and right now I want to tell you that I think all you men are wicked for the way you have been treating him! Here he is away out here, a stranger in a strange land, and simply because he is above the vulgar horseplay so popular around here, you ostracize him. Because his grammar and dress is perfect he is a pariah! Don't you think he feels that? Isn't he human the same as the rest of you? Why—why, if he were a woman, all the girls would have helped and encouraged him and made him welcome in any gathering while he was here. Don't you think it hurt when you broke up that poker party last night when he came in? Or when he was deliberately excluded from that hunting trip by that wretched Eddie Duke? Or any of the—the mean, petty, little things you have done to him—all of you—since he's been here? Oh, you men are horrid!" She gathers up her skirts and flashes Scanlan a look, "I thought *you*, at least, were different!" she whispers—and trips into the picture!

For about three minutes the Kid stands lookin' after her without sayin' a word. He acts like he has stopped one with his chin!

"The big English stiff!" he busts out finally. "What does he mean by comin' over here and gettin' me in a jam with my girl? I'll *get* that bird, though, believe me!"

"What are you gonna do?" I says.

"I'm gonna take that solemn-faced simp back of the African Desert and give him a chance at the welterweight title!" he snorts. "I'll wallop that bird till he'll wish he had stayed over in dear old England and—"

"Stoppa!" comes a voice from the back of us, and we look around into the muzzles of two automatics. On the other end of them was Tony!

"I hear everyt'ing!" he snarls, wavin' the guns and glarin' at us. "I hear everyt'ing!"

The Kid looks at the guns and coughs, kinda nervous. I was glancin' at friend Tony, myself.

"Ain't that nice!" I remarks, feelin' my way carefully.

"What you mean?" snarls the ex-"No spika da Engleesh."

"Bein' able to hear everything," I explains, thinkin' to humour him. "I'll bet right now you're listenin' to a little spicy scandal at some King's palace, eh?"

"Don't got funny!" he warns me.

"Ha! ha!" snickers the Kid. "Where d'ye get that got funny stuff?"

"What'sa that?" yells Tony, whirlin' on him and shovin' the guns under his nose.

The Kid gets pale and shuffles back a few steps.

"No spika da Engleesh!" he pipes, holdin' up his hand.

"Pah!" grunts Tony, registerin' disgust. "Me—I laugh at you! All the tima you talk 'bout Meester Van Ness, I standa rightta here with the ear wide open. You no feexa nobody—maybe Tony he'sa feexa you! I hear you say you no lika Meester Van Ness because he'sa no laugha. Sure, he'sa laugha—but not all the tima on the streeta like crazee fel'. When Meester Van Ness—ah, he'sa granda man—when he'sa wanna laugha, he'sa go home, to he'sa rooma, shutta the door and standa in the corner. Then he'sa a laugha ha! ha! ha! ho! ho! ho!—lika that! That'sa lasta heem all day!"

"Oh, Lady!" says the Kid, holdin' his side. "Can you tie that?" He looks over and sees Van Ness in a clinch with Miss Vincent—and son, you could see the muscles rollin' under his coat sleeves. "Look at the big, ignorant boob now!" he howls.

"Ignoranta!" hisses Tony. "Whata you mean, ignoranta? Seven difference language thisa granda Meester Van Ness he'sa speak! He'sa teacha everybody—joosta lika wan college!"

"Why don't you get him to teach you Eyetalian then, Stupid?" sneers the Kid. "You're a fine thing to luck your way past Ellis Island when you can't even tell me what *Bomb Germo* means!"

"Don't got funny!" warns Tony. "What gooda now for you be fighting champion for the world, eh? Leetle Tony he'sa standa here calla you names and what can you do, eh? Nothing—joosta nothing! Champion, eh? Ha, ha, ha! Don't maka me laugha, Meester Fightaire!" He shoves the gun in the Kid's face and snarls, "Now!" he says. "Tella Tony you feela sorry for soaka heem in jaw!"

The Kid bites his lip and edges in a bit. Right away I got sorry for Tony!

"I'm sorry!" sneers Scanlan slowly. "Awful sorry—just thinkin' of it has got me all broke up. I meant to let you have it on the beak, but I'll make up for it now!"

He looks over Tony's shoulder suddenly and yells. "Hey, don't throw that!"

If they had rehearsed the act, Tony couldn't have fallen

for the plant any harder. He twists his neck around to look back like the Kid figured and Scanlan started one from his left ankle. It caught Tony right on the button—which in English is the point of the chin—and Tony gives a imitation of a seal. He took a dive!

While we're takin' him away from his artillery, I look up and there's Van Ness lookin' down at us and frownin'. He reaches inside that Roman toga thing he's wearin' and comes out with a round piece of glass which he balances on one eye.

"Ah—I say!" he pipes, glarin' at the Kid. "This is getting jolly annoying, my man. It appears that every time we meet, you have just committed a murderous assault upon my dresser! Since you are the—ah—champion fighter of the universe, why do you not joust with more of its inhabitants and not center your activities upon one who knows nothing of the art of self-defense?"

The Kid grunts, takin' away Tony's guns and removin' a couple of them long banana knives from his clothes. Meanwhile, the daredevil dresser is showin' no more signs of life than a sleepin' alligator, so I figured it was about time to pull a little first aid stuff. I turned him over on his back and took off his coat, grabbin' it by the bottom and holdin' it up. They was a sudden crash and—Sweet Cookie! A lot of things fell on the ground, among 'em bein' one set of brass knuckles, one blackjack, two more guns, a thing that looked like a bayonet, five boxes of cartridges, a small bottle of nitro-glycerine and three sticks of dynamite! The last two fell in the folds of the coat, or we'd all have gone away from there. Tony's master looks at the layout with his eyes stickin' so far out of his head you could have knocked 'em off with a cane.

Scanlan eyes him and laughs.

"This is the bird which don't know nothin' about self-defense, eh?" he grins, pointin' to Tony. "Well, if he'd been in Belgium a few years ago, I bet the Germans would never have got through!"

"Oh, I say!" gasps Van Ness. "This is a bit of a shock! Why the fellow is a walking arsenal!"

"He's more like a sleepin' fort, now!" I says, pointin' to Tony on the turf.

"Look at the chances you been takin' havin' a guy like that fasten your garters and so forth," pipes Scanlan. "You ought to thank us for exposin' him!"

Then Tony comes to life and havin' helped him down, the Kid helps him up.

"*Sapristi*!" remarks Tony, glarin' at him. "You bigga stiffa! Sometime Tony he'sa feexa you for dis! Whata you hitta me with?"

"I think it was a left hook," the Kid tells him, rubbin' his chin, like he ain't sure.

"Aha!" snarls Tony. "I know you never hit with your feest sooch a punch! Don't got funny with me any more! I wanna tella you, you keepa up knock it down Tony every fiva, tena, fifteen minootes and some time Tony he'sa got mad! When Tony he'sa got mad—" He stops and makes a terrible face at me and the Kid, "—when Tony he'sa got mad, something she'sa gotta fall!—dat'sa all!"

"Well, you been doin' all the fallin' so far," I says, "and —"

"Ah—I say!" butts in Van Ness—and Tony sees him for the first time, I guess, because he shivered and got pale. "I say," he goes on, takin' a slant at Tony through the trick eyeglass, "just what does this mean, Antonio? Why are you walking about with this extraordinary collection of weapons on your person?" He points his finger at the munitions on the ground, and Tony's eyes follows his. At the same time he makes a little clickin' noise in his throat and jumps for the pile.

"Where is she the gooda carbolic acid?" he snarls. "And whosa taka my eleven incha stiletto?"

"How dare you ignore my question!" thunders Van Ness. "What are you doing with all those weapons? Answer me!"

"'Scuse a me!" says Tony, makin' a bow and takin' off his hat. "I getta them for my brudda!"

"Where's your brother?" asks the Kid. "In Russia?"

"'Sno use *you* talka to me!" growls Tony, "I no talka back. Sometime Tony he'sa getta mad and then—"

"Come, come!" interrupts Van Ness, kinda sharp. "The weapons—what of them?"

"'Scuse a me!" bows Tony with another smile. "My brudda he'sa live in Santa Francisco. He'sa fina fel'—my brudda. He'sa name Joe. He'sa come this countree five years ago, no fren's, no spika da Engleesh, no nothing! They putta heem in the basement of the sheepa wit' coupla thousand other fel' from seventy-six other countree. One fel' say my Joe he'sa no be able to leava the sheepa at—at—what you call? I don't know—I teenk maybe Chicago, Pennsylvania, Coney Island—I don't know joosta now! Anyhow thisa fel' say Joe he'sa no be able to leava the sheepa wherever he'sa wanna go—eef he'sa got no money, you 'stanna me? Joe he'sa tank dis kinda fel', say coupla nica prayer for heem and then everybody she'sa a maka sleepa. Joe he'sa get up and taka four hundred dollar from thisa nica fel'— whosa sleepa lika he'sa dead—so Joe he'sa be able to leeva the sheepa! He'sa a smarta fel', eh? That'sa Joe. He'sa my brudda!"

"Oh, Lady!" says the Kid. "What was you takin' him the ammunition for?"

"Don't spika to me!" snorts Tony. "I no answera you! I tella Meester Van Ness. He'sa my boss. He'sa fina fel', too— joosta lika my brudda!"

"How dare you!" splutters Van Ness, his face as red as a ale-hound's nose. "What do you mean by that?"

"'Scuse a me!" says Tony. "Don't get mad for Tony. No spika da Engleesh very gooda—maybe I maka meestake! Joe he'sa writa me come over Santa Francisco queek, because he'sa gotta the trouble wif he'sa landlord. Disa fel' he'sa a wanta da rent maybe, I don't know, but Joe he'sa wanta me bring something so he'sa can feex disa fel' nex' time he come around, you 'stanna me? He say he'sa a bigga fel'—tougha nut! Yesterday I go out and getta wan gun for Joe. Then I teenk maybe that ain't enough for poor leetle Joe against thisa bigga stiffa landlord, so I stoppa drugga store, hardaware, meata store, five, six, sevena place and get somet'ing for Joe he'sa feex landlord. Then I hear thisa fel' say he'sa gonna feexa *you*!" Tony swings around and points at the Kid. "Tony he'sa don't care if thisa bigga stiffa he's a champion for the world. Tony he's a gotta knifa, gun, dynamite, carbolic acida, everything for fighta. I talka to heem sweeta and he'sa knocka me down wit' a hook! While I sleepa on the dirt, somebody she'sa taka my gooda carbolic acida and stiletto I getta for Joe!"

"Oh, Lady!" yells the Kid, slappin' me on the back. "This guy is a riot!"

"You may go to the hotel, Antonio," says Van Ness, "and await me there. I am surprised and grieved at your beastly conduct!"

Tony hands Van Ness a gun and the bottle of nitro-glycerine.

"Alla right!" he says. "Tony he'sa go. But watcha this two fel' they wanna feexa you. The little fel' you can shoota—but the bigga stiffa whosa knocka me down, he'sa needa more than that! Taka thisa bottle and throw it at heem harda. That'sa blow heem away so far, it taka four thousand dollar for heem to come back on sheepa, thirda class!"

Van Ness puts the gun and the nitro in Tony's pocket.

"Begone, sir!" he says. "I'll jolly well attend to you later!"

Tony gathers up his junk and throwin' a last glare at me and the Kid, beats it.

Van Ness turns to the Kid, stickin' the eyeglass back in the toga.

"Ah—and now, Scanlan," he says, "will you be good enough to explain the cause of the—ah—bitter animosity you have for me?"

The Kid frowns and scratches his head.

"Somebody has been kiddin' you," he tells him. "I ain't got *nothin'* for you! Where d'ye get that animosity thing?"

Van Ness sighs so hard it like to blowed our hats off.

"It is beastly plain to me," he says, "that I am about as popular in Film City as a cloudburst at a picnic! I am snubbed, ridiculed, vulgarly and subtly insulted! Also I am white and human and—ah—I must confess it has penetrated my skin. *You* are particularly bitter against me—why?"

The Kid studies him for a minute.

"Listen!" he answers finally. "Are you on the level with this? D'ye really wanna know, or are you simply askin' me so's you can pull one of them witty remarks on the way I answer you —*and get walloped on the beak*?"

Van Ness did somethin' then I never seen him do before and only once afterward. *He grinned*! The Roman toga fell off his shoulders, and he leans over with his hands on his hips. On the level, his whole face seemed to change! And then—

Oh, boy!

"Listen, guy!" pipes this big, dignified whatnot. "I'm on the level, all right and I want the lowdown on this thing, d'ye make me?" (Me and the Kid nearly went dead on our feet listenin'.) "As for wallopin' me on the beak, well—you may be welterweight champion out here, but if you start anything with *me*, I'll remove you from the title, d'ye get that?"

Woof!

The Kid and me falls back against a rock, fightin' for air!

"Oh, Lady!" whispers the Kid, fannin' himself with his hat. "Did you hear what I did?"

"Call me at seven!" I gasps.

"Well—?" drawls Van Ness, lookin' us over.

"They's just one thing I'd like to know," murmurs the Kid, wipin' his forehead with my handkerchief in the excitement. "What part of dear old England was *you* born in?"

Van Ness grins some more.

"Brooklyn!" he says, jerkin' out the eye glass again and stickin' it on his eye. "Surely, my man," he goes on, with that old silly stare of his; "surely you have heard of jolly old Brooklyn— what?"

"I know it well!" says the Kid. "It's on the wrong end of the bridge! But where d'ye get the 'my man' thing? And what have you been goin' around like a Swiss duke or somethin', when it turns out you're only a roughneck from Brooklyn? You wanna know why you don't belong, and don't fit in here, eh? Well, you big hick, where d'ye get that Sedate Sam stuff?" He slaps Van Ness on the arm. "Why in the Hail Columbia don't you bust out and giggle now and then, hey?"

"Why don't I?" snarls Van Ness, "Don't you think I'd *like* to? Don't you think I would if I could, you boob?"

"Would if you *could*?" repeats the Kid. "What's the matter—have you got lockjaw?"

"No!" roars Van Ness, so sudden that we both sidestepped. "No! Not lockjaw, worse! *Dignity*!"

"Have you give the mud baths at Hot Springs a play?" I asks.

"Stop it!" he sneers. "Cease that small time comedy! I'm the most dignified person in the world—the undisputed champion! I'm Frowning Frank and Imposing Ike rolled into one. It hurts me more than it does you, but I can't help it! I fail to remember the last time I enjoyed a hearty laugh and I know it will be a darned long space before I'll snicker again. My laugher has gone unused for so long that it's atrophied and won't work. I've tried warming it up by going home at night and guffawing before the mirror, but the result is only a mirthless giggle—a ghostly chortle! Of course, I wouldn't dare attempt to laugh in public!"

"Do what?" asks the Kid.

"Laugh!" answers Van Ness bitterly. "I can't even let myself think of doing it—why, it would ruin me! My dignity is all I have. It's my stock in trade and without it I would lose my income! Were I to unbend and shatter the air with harmless cachinnation, it would be thought at once that I had been drinking!" He stopped and sighed some more. "It began ten years ago," he goes on. "I was playing small parts in a stock company and one week I was cast for a Roman senator. Being anxious to make good, I made that noble so dignified that the local critics dismissed the play with a few paragraphs and gave half a column to my stately bearing! That started it, and from that time I've played nothing but Romans, kings, governors, cardinals and similar roles, calling for my infernal talent in the one direction. Mechanically I grew to playing them *on and off*, yet all the time within me burns the desire to do rough and tumble, yes, by Heaven, slapstick comedy! But alas, I lack the moral courage to throw off the yoke!"

"Well, Mister Van Ness—" I begins, when the silence begun to hurt, "I—"

"Not Van Ness!" he interrupts. "The name is as false as my manner! My name is Fink, Eddie Fink, and please don't add the Mister. When a lad I had a nickname, but, alas, I—"

"What was it?" butts in the Kid.

He hesitates.

"Well, it was rather frivolous," he says. "As indeed I was myself—a happy, carefree youth! The boys called me Foolish— Foolish Fink!" He throws out his chest like he just realized how he had been honored at the time.

Me and the Kid both had a coughin' fit.

"Let's go over to Montana Bill's," I says, when I thought it was safe to look up, "and we'll talk it over."

"Yeh!" chimes in the Kid. "Over a tray of private stock!"

He laughs and slaps alias Van Ness on the shoulder. "Cheer up! Foolish Fink, will you have a little drink? Woof, woof! I'm a poet!"

"Thanks!" says Van Ness. "But I'm on the wagon. I stopped drinking five years ago, because under the influence of alcohol I've been known to act the fool!"

"You ain't the only one!" says the Kid. "Anyhow I never touch it myself and Johnny here only uses it on his hair! But come on over—you can have your pants pressed or take a shine, I'm gonna buy, and you might as well get in on it. Bill's got a laughin' hyena in a cage outside, and maybe you could get him to rehearse you!"

About a week after that, the society bunch in Frisco comes over to Film City to act in a picture for the benefit of the electric fan fund for Greenland, or somethin' like that. About fifty of the future corespondents, known to the trade as the younger set, blows over in charge of a dame who had passed her thirty-sixth birth and bust day when Napoleon was a big leaguer. She had did well by herself though and when dressed for the street, they was harder things to look at than her. Also, when her last husband died, he left her a bankroll that when marked in figures on paper looked like it was the number of Southerners below Washington. A little bit of a guy, which turned around when you yelled "G. Herbert Gale" at him, breezed over with her and at first I had him figured as a detective seekin' divorce evidence, because he stuck to that dame like a cheap vaudeville act does to the American flag. He trailed a few paces behind her everywhere she went, callin' her "Mrs. Roberts-Miller" in public and "Helen Dear" when he figured nobody was listenin'. It was easy to see that he had crashed madly in love with this charmer, but as far as she was concerned they was nothin' stirrin'.

Except that G. Herbert was inclined to be a simp, he wasn't a bad guy at that. He mixed well and bought freely, although he was riveted to the water wagon himself. He bragged to me in fact that the nearest he ever come to alcohol in his life was once when he used it to clean his diamonds.

But G. Herbert was the guy that invented the ancient and honorable order of village cut-ups. I never asked him what the G stood for in his name, I guessed it the first day he was in our midst. It meant "Giggle!" This here Herbert person was a laughin' fool! The first time I talked with him I thought I was cheatin' myself by only bein' Scanlan's manager. I figured I ought to be in vaudeville knockin' 'em dead for five hundred a week, because G. Herbert roared at everything I said. He screamed with mirth at all the old ones and had hysterics over three or four witty remarks I remembered from a show I seen the night of the Johnstown flood. I thought, of course, it was the way I put the stuff over, and I was just gonna give the Kid my fare-you-well, when I seen G. Herbert standin' by a practical undertakers shop that was fixed up for a fillum. The little simp was standin' over a coffin laughin' his head off!

That cured me, but him and the Kid become great little pals. I found out later it was on account of G. Herbert snickerin' at the Kid's comedy. Scanlan hadn't discovered it was a habit with this guy, and he claimed here was a feller that knowed humor when he seen it.

One afternoon I see Scanlan and Miss Vincent whisperin' together like yeggmen outside a postoffice. They called me over, and the Kid tells me that the society bunch was gonna leave us flat on the midnight train, and before they blowed, Potts was gonna give 'em a dinner and dance. All the movie crowd was to mix with Frisco's four hundred, so's that both could enjoy the experience and say they took a chance once in their lives.

But the thing that was botherin' Miss Vincent—(Some dame, that! She was the world's champion woman, believe me!) The thing that worried her was G. Herbert and Helen Dear, alias Mrs. Roberts-Miller. Likin' 'em both, Miss Vincent wanted to hurl 'em together for good and all before the train pulled out.

It seems the only objection the dame had to G. Herbert was the fact that he couldn't keep from laughin'. She had him figured as a eighteen-carat simp and frequently told him so, addin' that she could never marry a man who was shy on dignity. Then she gets a flash at our old pal Jason Van Ness or Eddie Fink, as he claimed, and she fell so hard for him she liked to broke her neck! Here was the only original Sedate Sam! Here was the guy she was willin' and anxious to lead to the altar and then to the old safe deposit vault! He was so handsome! So dignified! Such a splendid actor! That's the stuff she was always handin' poor little G. Herbert and askin' him why *he* wasn't like that? G. Herbert would shake his head, giggle, and say he didn't know why, but he'd ask his parents.

Van Ness couldn't see Helen Dear with opera glasses. He told me he hated 'em stout, and, if possible, had figured on weddin' somebody within ten years of his age—either way. I then felt it my duty to inform him that her bankroll was stouter than she was. He goes into high speed on the dignity thing and sets sail for Helen Dear like a bloodhound after a nigger. He didn't want to look like a vulgar fortune hunter, he claimed, but he figured if he could get his fingers on a piece of Helen's dough, he could bribe G. Herbert to teach him the art of laughin'.

The Kid tells Miss Vincent to forget about the thing, and he would guarantee that G. Herbert and Helen Dear went away threatenin' to marry each other. She said she'd leave the matter in our hands and held hers out. I shook it and Scanlan kissed it—a trick he stole from Van Ness.

The dinner and dance that night was a knockout! Film City is lit up like a plumber used to be on Saturday night, and the inhabitants is dressed like the people that poses for the ads of any cigarette over fifteen cents a pack. As usual, Miss Vincent had the rest of the dames lookin' like sellin' platers in stake race and, believe me, some of them society girls would have worried Venus. The Kid was so swelled up because she kept within easy call all night that he forgot his promise to fix up G. Herbert with Helen Dear. The latter, as we remark at the laundry, was closer to Van Ness all night than the ocean is to the beach, and it looked like the Kid was gonna have a tough time breakin' 'em up.

Along around eleven, Miss Vincent calls Scanlan aside and reminds him that he had better start workin' for G. Herbert, because they would all be beatin' it for the train in a hour. She also give out that, if he didn't make good, she was off him for life. Scanlan bows—another trick he copped from Van Ness—and takes me away down at the end of the lawn to dope somethin' out.

I tripped over what I thought at first was a dead body and me and the Kid props it up in the light.

"Ha, ha!" it says. "Tony he'sa laugha at you! Tony he'sa laugha at everybody! *Bomb Germo*! thisa fel' tella me—ha, ha, ha!"

The Kid grunts in disgust, lets go and Tony bounces back on the lawn.

"Stewed to the scalp!" says Scanlan. "Frisk him!"

I run my hands over Tony and bring forth a bottle of gin and another one of bourbon. The Kid looks 'em over, finally stickin' 'em both in his coat pocket.

"Come on!" he tells me. "They's no use hangin' around here. If I don't get back there, some of them Wealthy Willies that have been wishin' all night will be one-steppin' with Miss Vincent!"

"But how about G. Herbert?" I says.

"He's got my best wishes!" growls the Kid. "He's a nice little feller, but that's the best I can do. What d'ye think I am—Cupid?"

"Well, gimme the alcohol then!" I says. "You ain't gonna fall off the wagon are you, when—"

"Shut up, Stupid!" he butts in. "I wouldn't take a drink of this stuff for what Rockefeller gets for overtime! I want to get it away from that wop, so's he'll have somethin' to moan about when he wakes up."

We went back to the party, and a couple of dames standin' at the punch bowl calls to the Kid. He always was a riot with the women! Helen Dear is there with Van Ness, and he's got to where he's pattin' her hand, while G. Herbert stands in back of 'em lookin' like he wished he had some nails to bite.

I come to a table and there's Miss Vincent sittin' alone and she motions me to sit down with her—so's my back would hide her from the rest of the bunch. She says a little bit of society went a long ways with her, and where was the Kid? Before I can answer her along comes Helen Dear and she plumps down at the table and starts to tell us what a magnificent man Mister Van Ness was. She claims she never seen such a perfect gentleman in her life. I liked to snickered out loud at the disappointed way she pulled that one and then the Kid, G. Herbert and Van Ness suddenly comes around a tree and joins the party.

Scanlan winks at Miss Vincent, and she looks at him inquiringly, but he just shakes his head. I noticed that G. Herbert looked kinda sad, and he must have put his giggler away because he just sat lookin' down at the ground. Van Ness is full of life—I never seen him so cheerful—so I figured that while them and the Kid was alone, Van Ness must have told 'em that Helen Dear had proposed or accepted him.

Finally, Helen Dear looks at her wrist watch and says she'll have to tear herself away, because the train leaves in fifteen minutes. She wastes five of that throwin' soulful looks at Van Ness and he give back as good as he got. G. Herbert offers to get her wraps, comin' to life long enough to make the request, but Helen Dear gives him a sneerin' look and says there was servants there for that purpose. It was a terrible throwdown, and Van Ness nearly grinned, but G. Herbert gamely tried a giggle that sounded like the squeak of a stepped-on rat.

While Helen Dear is gettin' into a coat that couldn't have

cost a nickel under five thousand bucks, the Kid gets up and calls Van Ness and G. Herbert aside. They was gone about five minutes. When they came back, Helen Dear is just puttin' on her hat and suddenly the thing slips out of her hands and slides down over one eye.

Then—excuse me a minute, I'm in convulsions! I'll never forget it if I live to see Bryan vote against prohibition! There's Helen Dear gettin' red in the face and strugglin' with that hat and —

"Ha, ha, ha, ha!" shrieks Van Ness—*the guy that had lost his laugher*!—"Ha, ha, ha, ha!" he yells, holdin' the chair so's he can stand up and pointin' at Helen's hat. "You ought to go in vaudeville!" he hollers. "You'd be a riot with that act! Ha, ha, ha, ha, ha, ha!"

Miss Vincent gasps, the Kid grins, and I all but fainted. Here's this guy laughin' his head off for the first time in ten years and—look at the time he picked to do it! Sweet Cookie!

Helen Dear turns eighteen shades of red and fights for her breath like a fish when you drag it over the side of the boat. Then up steps little G. Herbert. His eyes is kinda glassy, but his face is set and hard. His spine is as straight as a flag pole and he sticks a piece of glass over one eye, just like Van Ness used to do! Dignity? Why he could have took Van Ness when that guy was right—*and give him lessons*!

"What does this mean, sir!" he says, walkin' up to Van Ness who is holdin' his sides and fallin' off the chair. Laugh? That bird was in hysterics!

"Ha, ha, ha!" bellers Van Ness. "Get a couple of good camera men quick! Ha, ha, ha, ha! It looks like she got hit with a pie!"

"You infernal idiot!" roars G. Herbert. "How dare you laugh at this lady?"

"Oh, boy!" answers Van Ness, finally rollin' off his chair. "Ha, ha, ha, ha!"

"Come, Herbert!" pipes Helen. "We will go back together and my answer is Yes! Thank Heaven that man stands exposed in his true character!"

"Thas' right!" nods Herbert, waggin' his head and glarin' at all of us. "C'mon—hic—Cmon, M' dear!"

Somethin' comes staggerin' up and grabs the Kid by the arm. It was Tony.

"Aha!" he yells. "Who'sa taka my bottle gin, bottle bourbon? *Sapristi*! You bigga stiffa, I—"

The Kid gives him a slow straight arm, and Tony goes over the table backwards, landin' right beside his master.

"No spika da Engleesh!" says Scanlan, as Tony disappears.

I grabbed him by the arm.

"Show me them bottles," I says, gettin' wise in a flash.

The Kid takes out two *empty* non-refillables and tosses 'em in the grass.

"My!" he says, dreamily. "How that little guy went to it!"

Toot! Toot! Toot! goes the Santa Fe flier pullin' out with G. Herbert and Helen Dear.

"Ha, ha, ha, ha, ha, ha, ha—ho, ho, ho, ho!" screams Van Ness from under the table. "She promised—ha, ha, ha! to cheer me up—hic—ha, ha, ha! and she—hic—certainly—ha, ha, ha!—made good!"

CHAPTER VI
THE UNHAPPY MEDIUM

They may be such a thing as a ghost, but I don't believe it! At the same time, I'm willin' to admit that my feelin's in the matter ain't gonna prove the ruin of the haunted house promoters. They's a whole lot of things which I look on as plain and simple bunk, that the average guy studies at college. But the reason I say they *may* be, is because when me and Kid Scanlan come back East this year we stopped off somewheres in the hurrah for prohibition part of the country and was showed over what the advertisin' matter admitted to be the greatest bakery in the world.

I think them ad writers was modest fellers. That joint was not only the world's greatest bakery, it was the world's greatest *anything*!

I never really knowed a thing about bread, except that you put butter on it, until I give that place the up and down.

What I don't know about the staff of life now would never get you through Yale. I might go farther than that and come right out with the fact that I have become a abandoned bread fiend and got to have it or I foam at the mouth, since I seen how it was made at this dough foundry.

A accommodatin' little guy took hold of me and the Kid and showed us all over the different machine shops where this here bread was mixed, baked and what-notted for the trade. Our charmin' guide must have come from a family of auctioneers and circus barkers and he never heard of no sums under ten or eleven thousand in his life. He knowed more about figures than Joe Grady, who once filled in a summer with a Russian ballet, and he had been wound up and set to deliver chatter at the rate of three words a second, provided the track was fast and he got off in front. He talked with his whole body, waggin' his head, movin' his arms and shufflin' his feet. When he got warmed up and goin' good, he pushed forward at you with his hands like he was tryin'

124

to insert his chatter right into you.

He leads us to a spot about half a mile from where we come in, holds up his hands to Heaven, coughs, blows his nose and gives a little shiver.

"Over there!" he bellers, without no warnin'. "Over there is our marvelous, mastadon, mixin' shop. We use 284,651 pounds of scrupulously sifted and freshly flavored flour, one million cakes of elegant yeast and 156,390 pounds of bakin' powder each and every year! We employ 865 magnificent men there and they get munificent money. We don't permit the use of drugs, alcoholics, tobacco or unions! The men works eight easy hours a delightful day, six days a week and they are happy, hardy and healthy! Promotion is regular, rapid and regardless! Our employees is all loyal, likable and Lithuanians! They own their own cottages, clothes and chickens, bein' thrifty, temperate and —"

"Tasty!" I yells. I couldn't, keep it in no longer!

"What?" snaps the little guy, kinda sore.

"Lay off, Stupid!" says the Kid to me, with a openly admirin' glance at the runt. "Go on with your story," he nods to him. "Never mind Senseless, here, I'm gettin' every word of it!"

The little hick glares at me and points to a shack on the left.

"Over there," he pipes. "Over there is our shippin' plant where the freshly finished and amazingly appetizin' loaves are carefully counted and accurately assembled! For this painstakin' performance we employ 523 more men. None but the skilled, superior and—and—eh—Scandinavian are allowed in that diligent department, and each and every day a grand, glorious total of ten thousand lovely loaves is let loose with nothin' missin' but the consumer's contented cackle as he eagerly eats! We even garnish each loaf with a generous gob of Gazoopis— our own ingenuous invention—before they finally flitter forth! Would you like to see the shop?"

"I certainly wish *I* could sling chatter like that!" answers the Kid with a sigh. "But I guess it's all in the way a guy was brung up. Gobs of generous Gazoopis!" he mutters, turnin' the words over in his mouth like they was sweet morsels. "Gobs of generous Gazoopis! Oh, boy!"

The little guy throws out his chest and bows with a "I-thank-you" look all over his face. He got me sore just watchin' him. Y'know that runt hated himself!

"Say!" I says to him. "If all that stuff you claim for this roll foundry is on the level, it must take a lot of dough to run it, eh?"

"Are you tryin' to kid me?" he sneers.

"No!" I comes back. "But speakin' of bakeries, I'd sacrifice my sacred silk socks for a flash at them skilled Scandinavians assemblin' that bread, before I move on to nasty New York!"

The Kid slaps me on the back and grins.

"Go on, Foolish!" he says. "You got this bird on the ropes!" He turns to the runt. "All I want," he goes on, "is one peep at them likable Lithuanians—can I git that?"

"You guys is as funny as pneumonia to me!" snorts the little guy, gettin' red in the face. "That stuff may pass for comedy in Yonkers or wherever you hicks blowed in from, but it don't git no laugh outa me! D'ye wanna see this shop or don't you—yes or no?"

"Let's go!" I tells him. "You got me all worked up about it!"

"Same here!" says the Kid. "I only wish I could talk like you can, but I guess it's a gift, ain't it?"

The little guy grunts somethin' and nods for us to fall in behind him, and we lock step along till we come to another joint from which was issuin' what I'll lay eight to five was all the noise in the world. How they ever gathered it up and got it in the buildin' I don't know, but I do know it was there! If you'd take a bowlin' alley on Turnverein night, a boiler factory workin' on a rush order and the battle of Gettysburg, wind 'em up and set 'em all off at once, you might get a faint idea of how the inmates of that buildin' was ruinin' the peace and quiet of the surroundin' country. A dynamite explosion in the next block would have attracted as much attention as a whisper in a steamfittin' shop.

"I thought the war was all over!" hollers the Kid, holdin' his ears. "Has the police been tipped off about this?"

"What d'ye mean the police?" screams back the runt. "That there is the mixin' and bakin' shop."

"Yeh?" I cuts in. "Well, I don't know what them skilled Scandinavians of yours is at, but, believe me, they're *tryin'* all right!"

The runt sneers at us.

"You must be a fine pair of hicks!" he says. "D'ye mean to say you never heard of the Eureka Mixin' and Bakin' machine?"

"I can hear it now, all right!" I tells him, noddin' to the buildin' where the boilermakers was havin' a field day, "but—"

"Sufferin' salmon, what boobs!" he interrupts me. Then he gives us both the once over and starts his sneerer workin' again. "Say!" he asks me. "Who d'ye like to win the battle of Santiago and d'ye think Lincoln will git elected again?"

"I don't know," I comes back. "I'm gonna vote for Jefferson myself!" I looks him right in the eye. "I think Washington is a sucker to hang around Valley Forge all winter, don't you?" I asks him.

"Couple of small time cut-ups, eh?" he says, shakin' his head. "Where d'ye come from?"

"New York," the Kid tells him, "and listen—will you do me a favor and let's hear some more about them likable Lithuanians and gobs of generous Gazoopis?"

"I figured you come from some hick burg like New York," says the runt, ignorin' the Kid's request. "I can spot a guy from New York ten miles away! He knocks Brooklyn, thinks walkin' up Broadway is seein' life, was born in Memphis and is the only thing that keeps the mail order houses in Oshkosh from goin' to the wall! New Yorkers, eh?" he winds up with another insultin' sneer. "I got you!"

"Gobs of generous Gazoopis!" mutters the Kid like he's in a trance. "Sweet Papa!"

The runt looks at him.

"How does *that* bird fool the almshouse?" he asks me.

I bent down so's I could whisper in the side of his little dome. Them skilled Scandinavians in the buildin' had gone crazy or else some of the night shift had come in with more boilers and things to hit 'em with.

"That's Kid Scanlan, welterweight champion of the world!" I hisses in his ear.

"Ha, ha!" laughs the runt. "That's who he'd *like* to be, you mean!"

"Our employees is all hale, hearty and hilarious!" grins the Kid at him. "We pay 'em off in money, music and mush! Wow!"

"If that big stiff is tryin' to kid me," begins the runt, gettin' red again, "he—"

"All right, all right!" I butts in quickly. "Don't let's have no violence. Show us what makes that shop go, and we'll grab the next rattler for New York. Y'know the Kid fights Battlin' Edwards on the twenty-first and—"

"Are you on the *level* with that stuff?" interrupts the runt, still lookin' at the Kid. "Is that really Kid Scanlan?"

I calls the Kid over.

"Kid," I says, "meet Mister—er—"

"Sapp," says the runt. "Joe Sapp!" He sticks out his hand. "I remember you now," he tells the Kid. "I seen you fight some tramp in Fort Wayne last year. I think you hit this guy with everything but the referee and that's why I like your work.

When *I* send in three bucks for a place to sit down at a box fight, I expect to see assault and batter and not the Virginia Reel! Why —"

"Not to give you a short answer," I butts in, "but how about the insane asylum over there?" I points to the buildin'. "Do we see that or don't we?"

Right away he straightens up and sticks his finger at it.

"It takes exactly twelve, temptin' minutes to completely compose and accurately assemble a loaf!" he shouts. "We never heard of waste, and efficiency was born in this factory. The only thing that loafs here is the bread! Each eager employee has his own particular part to perform and that accounts for the amazin' and awesome accuracy with which we bake the beautiful bread. Step this way!"

"Believe me!" says the Kid, "I wish I had a line of patter like that! 'Amazin' and awesome accuracy'!" he repeats. "Do you get that?"

Right then about a dozen dames and their consorts come breezin' in the main entrance. Offhand, they look like the hicks that gives the "Seein' New York" busses a play, and when the runt spots them he ducks and grabs my arm.

"C'mon!" he says. "Shake it up! If them boobs see me, I'll have to show 'em all over the plant! That's a gang of them Snooks' Tourists, seein' the world for fourteen eighty-five a-piece, breakfast at hotel on third mornin' out and bus from train included! Most of them is wisenheimers from Succotash Crossin', Mo.; and they're out to see that they don't get cheated. They're gonna see everything like it says on the ticket, and some of 'em is ready to sue Snooks because they got somethin' in their eye from lookin' out the train window and missed eight telegraph poles and a water tank on account of it. The rest of them sits around knockin' everything on general principles and claimin' the thing is a fake. Then there'll be one old guy in the party with a trick horn he holds to his ear, and, when I get all through tellin' 'em about the mixin' shop, the deef guy will say, 'Hey? What was that about the airship again?' There will also be three veteran school-teachers which will want samples of the bread and hide out a couple of rolls on the side. And then one young married couple which started sayin' 'Wonderful!' when the train pulled out of the old home town and which has said nothin' else but that since! No, sir! I'm off them tourists—c'mon, sneak around here!"

He boldly walks into the buildin' where all the noise is comin' from, and not wantin' to act yellah before strangers we followed him in. They was a lot of things in there and if you ever make the town, Joe Sapp will show 'em to you. He has to, in order to eat. But the only thing I remember was the way them lovely, luxurious loaves was artistically assembled, and I'll remember that little item till the insurance company pays off!

They was a great, big machine in the middle of the floor and that was the thing that was makin' the bread and noise. A half dozen of them skilled Scandinavians stood away up on a gallery at one end and their job was of a pourin' nature. They was all dressed in white and wore little trick hats on which it said this, "No Human Hands Touch It." I didn't know whether it meant the skilled Scandinavians or the beautiful bread.

"The most marvelous, magnificent, mammoth invention of the age!" bawls the runt so's we could hear him over the noise. "Here is where the beautiful bread is blissfully baked by the wonderful workmen! This machine cost the sensational sum of half a million dollars, and its capacity is a trifle over five hundred finely finished luscious loaves each and every—"

That's all I heard because I went in a trance from watchin' the thing. I never seen nothin' like it before and I know darn well I never will again. Listen! Them skilled Scandinavians poured in raw wheat at one end of this here machine, and it come out the other end, steamin' hot bread! Some machine, eh? Not only that, but when it come out, it was baked, labelled, wrapped in oil paper and smellin' most heavenly from that generous gob of Gazoopis, as the runt said.

I dragged the Kid outside and we started for the railroad station without comment. As we passed out the door, we heard the runt screamin', probably thinkin' we was still there.

"One section reduces the wheat to flour, another mixes the dough, it passes on to the steam ovens and then what happens? *Bread*! Over here—"

The Kid stops all of a sudden, takes a hitch in his belt and looks back at the shop.

"Hell!" he says. "They *can't* make no bread like that!"

"You seen 'em do it, didn't you?" I asks him, although I was thinkin' the same thing myself.

"Even at that," he comes back, "I don't believe it!"

We walks on a little ways, and the Kid stops again.

"I certainly wish I could talk like that little runt!" he shoots out. "Take it from me, that bird is there forty ways. He's got Webster lookin' like a dummy!"

He keeps on mutterin' to himself as we breeze up to the station, and, when I lean over to get an earful I hear him sayin', "They're all simple, sassy and suckers! We feed 'em oranges, oatmeal and olives!"

So, as I said before, they *may* be such a thing as ghosts. After watchin' that bread bakin' machine at play I'll go further than that. There may be *anything*!

One day at the trainin' camp, a couple of weeks after we hit New York, a handler comes to me and says they's two guys outside that wants to see the Kid. I hopped out to take a flash at 'em, but the Kid has been reached, and when I come on the scene he's shakin' hands with 'em. One of these guys was dressed the way the public thinks bookmakers and con men doll up and he wore one of them sweet, trustin' innocent faces like you see on the villain in a dime novel. He looked to me like he'd steal a sunflower seed from a blind parrot.

But it was the other guy that was the riot to me.

He was tall and lanky, dressed all in black like the pallbearer the undertaker furnishes, and the saddest-lookin' boob I ever seen in my life! If he wasn't the original old Kid Kill-Joy, he was the bird that rehearsed him, believe me! Y'know just from lookin' at this guy, a man would get to thinkin' about his past life, the time he throwed the baby down the well when but a playful child, how old his parents was gettin' and the time Shorty Ellison run off with the red-headed dame that lived over the butcher's. You wished you had saved your money or somebody else's, suddenly findin' out that it was a tough world where a poor man didn't have a Chinaman's chance, and you wondered if death by drownin' was painful or not.

That's the way it made you feel when you just looked at this guy. Ever see one of 'em?

He had a trick of sighin'. Not just ordinary heaves, but deep, dark and gloomy sighs that took all the life out of whoever he sighed at. If they had that bird over in Europe, they never would have been no war, because when he started sighin', nobody would have had enough ambition left to fight. Every time he opened his mouth I thought he was gonna say, "Merciful Heaven help us all!" or somethin' like that. But he didn't. He just sighed.

The Kid tells me the riot of color was Honest Dan Leduc, and that he was the best behaved guy that ever spent a week end in Sing Sing, where he had gone every now and then to study jail conditions at the request of thirteen men, the same bein' a judge and a jury. The sad-lookin' boob was Professor Pietro Parducci, the well known medium.

"Medium what?" I says, when the Kid pulls that one.

The Kid frowns at me and turns to his new found friends.

"Don't mind Foolish here," he tells 'em, "he's got the idea that everything is crooked. He thinks the war was a frame-up for the movies, and the Kaiser got double-crossed, but he ain't a bad guy at that. He knows more about makin' money than a lathe hand at the mint." He jerks his thumb at Honest Dan and swings around on me. "This guy and me was brung up together," he explains, "and before I went into the fight game we was as close as ninety-nine and a hundred. He's been all over the world since then, he says so himself, but just now he's up against it. It seems he was runnin' a pool room on Twenty-Eighth Street and he give the wrong winner of the Kentucky Derby to the precinct captain. The next mornin' the captain give every cop in the station house a axe and Dan's address. His friend here is a now, whosthis and—"

Honest Dan pulls what I bet he thought was a pleasant smile. It reminded me more of a laughin' hyena.

"One minute!" he butts in. "My friend, the world-renowed Professor Parducci, is a medium, a mystic and a swami. He's the seventh son of a seventh son, born with a veil and spent two years in Indiana with the yogi. He can peer into the future or gaze back at the past. He is in direct communication with the spirits of the dear departed and as a crystal gazer and palmist he stands alone!"

"That's a great line of patter, Dan," says the Kid, "but we met a guy on the trip back that had the English language layin' down and rollin' over when he snapped his fingers. Generous gobs of Gazoopis and likable, loyal Lithuanians! Can you tie that?"

I was still lookin' over the gloomy guy with the name that sounded like a brand of olive oil, and I decided he was the bunk. I asked him could he tell my fortune, and he draws himself up and claims he's not in harmony just now. That was the tip-off to me, and I figures he has come out to take the Kid for his bankroll. I knowed he couldn't tell no fortunes the minute I seen him. He didn't look to me as if he could tell his own name, and I bet all the spirits he ever communicated with was called private stock. The end of his nose was as red as a four alarm fire and the back of his collar was all wore off from where he had kept throwin' back his head so's the saloon keepers could meet expenses. Honest Dan said he couldn't speak much English, so I guess he had stopped at "I'll have the same" and "Here's a go!"

Well, I had the right dope, because the next week the Kid goes down to the bank and draws out five thousand bucks to set Honest Dan and the professor up in business with. They was gonna open a swell fortune-tellin' joint on Fifth Avenue. I said the thing sounded crooked to me, and the Kid got sore and told me Honest Dan couldn't do nothin' like that, it wasn't in him. He showed me where Dan had always got time off for good conduct, no matter what jail he was in.

The professor brightens up for a minute when the Kid hands over the roll, but after that he went right back into the gloom again.

Honest Dan gives the Kid a receipt for the sucker money and him and his trick medium goes on their way. After a while, I forgot about 'em. The Kid fights Edwards and a couple of more tramps and knocks 'em all kickin' and we're just gonna grab one of them "See America Firsts" for the coast when some club promoter goes crazy and offers us ten thousand iron men to fight Joe Ryan. The Kid would have fought the Marines for half of that, so we run all the way to the club and signed articles whiles the guy that hung up the purse was still wishin' he had stayed on the wagon.

The Kid had got Professor Parducci to fix him up with a few love charms and owls' ears by which he was gonna make himself solid with Miss Vincent. In fact Scanlan fell so hard for the medium stuff that when the professor told him to get at all cost a lock of Miss Vincent's hair clipped at eighteen minutes after eleven on a rainy Sunday night, he writes out to her and asks her to send him a lock cut just that way!

When he wasn't pesterin' the professor on how to win the movie queen, he was goin' around mutterin', "Loyal, likeable

Lithuanians and generous gobs of Gazoopis!" until the newspaper guys wrote that Kid Scanlan would be a mark for the first good boy he fought, because like everybody else that was a sudden success, he had took to usin' stimulants which is only sold on a doctor's prescription. On the level, he'd git a wad of paper and sit around all night with a dictionary, writin' down all the words that begin with the same letter and then he'd git up and repeat that stuff for a hour.

One afternoon we went downtown to look over this joint run by Honest Dan and the professor. It was in one of them studio buildings on Fifth Avenue near Twenty-Eighth Street, and the rent they was payin' for it would have kept the army in rubber heels for six years. They's a long line of autos outside and the inmates was streamin' in and out of the place like a crowd goin' to see the beloved rector laid out. Some of the dames would be familiar to you, if you've been readin' the box scores in the latest divorce mêlées, or the lineup of the committee for the aid of the Esquimaux victims of the war.

We get in a elevator, and, floatin' up to the roof, walk down what would have been a fire trap on the East Side, and here we are at Professor Parducci's Temple of the Inner Star. A couple of West Indian hall boys, who's gag line was "Say-hib," lets us in. They was dressed in sheets and had towels twisted around their heads and smelled strongly of gin. Pretty soon Honest Dan comes out and shakes hands all around. Except for his face, you'd never know it was the same guy. His hair is brushed all the way back like the guys that poses for the underwear ads and he's dressed in a black suit that fit him better than most of his skin. In his shirt front they's a diamond that looked like a young arc light, and he had enough gems on his hands to make J. P. Morgan gnash his teeth.

He told me that him and the professor wasn't doin' no more business than a guy would do in Hades with the ice water concession, and that Barnum was wrong when he said they was a sucker born every minute. Honest Dan said *his* figures showed there was about two born every *second*.

He leads us into a great big hall that was filled with statues, pictures, rugs, sofas, women and fatheads. The furnishings of this joint would make Buckingham Palace look like a stable. It must have ruined the Kid's five thousand just to lay in scenery for that one room alone. The statues and pictures was nearly all devoted to one subject, and that was why should people wear clothes—especially women? The victims is all lollin' around on them plush sofas, drinkin' tea and lookin' like a ten-year-old kid at church or a guy waitin' in the doctor's office to find out if he's got consumption or chilblains. It was as quiet as a Sunday in Philadelphia and they was also a very strong smell of burnin' glue, which Honest Dan said was sacred incense that always had to be used by the professor before he could work.

Among the decorations was a very large dame sittin' over in a corner dressed within a inch of her life. I suppose she had ears, a neck and hands, but you couldn't tell right away whether she had or not, because them parts of her anatomy, as the feller says, was buried under a carload of diamonds. You could see by her face that at one time she had probably been a swell-lookin' dame, but them days was all over. Still, she was makin' a game try at comin' back, and from her complexion she must have been kept busy day and night openin' bottles and cans signed on the outside by Lillian Russell and etc.

This dame was havin' the best time of anybody in the joint. She was sittin' up very straight and solemn with both chins restin' in her glitterin' hands and from the look in her eyes some Sunday paper had just claimed she was the best lookin' woman in America and the like.

A guy wouldn't have to be no Sherlock Holmes to see that this was the bird that was bein' readied for the big killin' by Honest Dan and his trick professor. The rest of them was just what you might call the chorus.

Sittin' right beside the stout party was a kid that had just dropped in from the cover of a magazine. She was the kind of female that could come down to breakfast with the mumps and her hair in curl papers, fry the egg on the wrong side and yet make the lucky guy across the table go out whistlin' and pityin' his unwed friends. You know how them dames look when they have give some time to *dollin' up*, don't you? Well, this one had everything; take it from me, she was a knockout! She's tappin' the floor with a classy little foot and tryin' to see can she pull a silk handkerchief apart with her bare hands, the while registerin' this, "This-medium-thing-is-the-bunk-and-I-wish-I-was-out-of-here!"

I doped her as the stout dame's daughter, hittin' .1000 on the guess as I found out later.

"Well," whispers Honest Dan to the Kid, "what d'ye think of the place?"

"Some joint!" says the Kid. "Listen—I got a new one. The most magnificently, male mauler on earth! How's that—poor, eh?"

"What does it mean?" asks Honest Dan.

"It means *me*, Stupid!" pipes the Kid. "I'm havin' some cards made up with that on it. The sagacious, sanguine and scandalous Scanlan, welterweight walloper of the world! Where's the professor?"

"Sssh!" whispers Honest Dan. "Lay off that *professor* gag here. That's small town stuff—he's a mahatma now! He's in one of his silences, but if you keep quiet I'll take you around and show you how he works."

He takes us through a little door that leads into a dark room which was a steal on the old chamber of horrors at the Eden Musee. It was full of ghost pictures drawed by artists who had no use for prohibition, and they was plenty of skulls and stuff like that layin' around where they would do the most good. At the far end is a small wire gratin' with a Morris chair on the other side of it. Honest Dan explains that that's where the come-ons sit while the professor massages their soul. They never see him, Dan figurin' in that way it would be harder to pick the professor out at police headquarters when the district attorney got around to him. We hadn't been there a minute, when the curtain at the other end of the room opens and in blows the stout dame, floppin' down in the chair with a sigh as the professor pulls open the grate to feed her the oil. Dan pulls us back in the dark, and I notice she was so excited that she shook all over like a ten cent portion of cornstarch or Instant Desserto and her breath was comin' in short little gasps.

Honest Dan is takin' a inventory of the couple of quarts of diamonds she wore and figurin' the list price on his shirt cuffs. When he got through, he dug me in the ribs and says it looks like a big winter.

The professor starts to talk with a strong Ellis Island dialect, tellin' the dame that he's just been in a trance, give the sacred crystal the once over and took up her case with a few odd ghosts. The result was that a spirit which was in the know had just give him a tip that she was no less than the tenth regular reincarnation of Cleopatra, who did a big time act in one with a guy called Marc Anthony which was now doin' a single or had jumped to the movies or somethin' like that.

The stout dame gets up off the chair and waves her handkerchief.

"Merciful Heavens!" she remarks loudly. "I knew it!"

Then she pulls a funny fall and faints!

The professor hisses at Dan to get him a cigarette, and the West Indian hall boys drag the stout dame into the chair from which she had slipped followin' the professor's sure-fire stuff about Cleopatra. He snatches a few drags out of the cigarette before the dame comes to and when she does, he goes on and says yes she is Cleopatra, they ain't no doubt about that part of it and she must have noticed the strange power she had over men all her life, hadn't she? The stout dame sighs and nods her head. The professor then tells her that she has been in wrong and unhappy all her life, because she had never met her mate. The same bein' a big, husky, red-blooded cave man which would club her senseless and carry her off to his lair. Had she ever met anybody like that? The stout dame says not lately, but when poor Henry and her had first got wed he was a Saturday night ale-hound and once or twice he had—but never mind, she won't speak ill of the dead. The professor says he can see that nobody of the real big-league calibre has crossed her path as yet and that her husband's spirit had told him in confidence only the other day that one night he got to thinkin' what a poor worm he was to be married to Cleopatra, and it had been too much for his humble soul which bust.

The dame nods and starts to weep.

"Poor Hennerey!" she says. "He ain't stopped lyin' yet. I should never have wed him, but how did I know that my fatal beauty would prove his undoing?"

"Ain't that rich?" pipes Honest Dan in my ear.

The professor has a coughin' spell, and when he calmed himself, he says he has just got in touch with Marc Anthony and he's pullin' the wires to have him come back to earth so's their souls can be welded together again and if she will come back in a week, he'll be able to tell her some big news. He said it was bein' whispered around among the spirits that Marc Anthony was on earth now, eatin' his noble heart out because he couldn't find her.

Then he suddenly shuts the gate, and the dame staggers out, overcome with joy and the smell of that incense which would have made a glue factory quit. Honest Dan beats it around and opens the door for her. They wouldn't take a nickel off her then, because they was savin' her for the big play.

About a week after our visit to the Temple of the Inner Star, the Kid comes runnin' up to my room at the hotel one mornin' and busts in the door. He's got a newspaper in his hand

and he slams it down on the bed and kicks a innocent chair over on its side.

"I hope they give him eighty years!" he hollers.

"Who's your friend?" I asks him.

"Friend!" he screams. "Why, the big psalm-singin' stiff, I'll murder him!"

"They's just one thing I'd like to know, Kid," I says. "Who?"

"That cheap, pan-handlin' crook that Dan Leduc wished on me!" he yells. "That rotten snake I kept from dyin' in the gutter, that baby-stealin' rat which claims he's a medium! Professor Bunko—that's who!"

I grabbed up the paper and all over the front page is a picture of Miss Vincent. Underneath it says this,

"Famous Film Star Rumored Engaged to Millionaire."

"Well," I says, "what has this here social note got to do with the Professor?"

"What has a jockey got to do with horse-racin'?" bellers the Kid. "Why the big hick, I'll go down there and strangle him right out loud before them high-brow simps of his! I'll have him pinched and I hope he gets life! I'll—"

He went on like that for half an hour, and when he finally cools off he explains that the professor had guaranteed to dust off his charmers and charm Miss Vincent so hard that she wouldn't even give a pleasant smile to nobody but the Kid. All Scanlan had to do was follow the professor's dope and they'd be nothin' to it but slippin' the minister and payin' the railroad people for the honeymoon. The Kid had gone ahead and done like the professor said, startin' off with the letter requestin' a lock of her hair clipped at eleven eighteen on a rainy Sunday night. Then he telegraphed her to bathe her thumbs in hot oolong tea every Friday at noon and send him the leaves in a red envelope. He followed that up with a note demandin' a ring that she had first dipped in the juice of a stewed poppy, and then held in back of her while she said, "Alagazza, gazzopi, gazzami" thirteen times.

I guess the professor overplayed the thing a bit, because the only action the Kid got was a short note from Miss Vincent in which she said that as long as he had started right in to drink the minute he hit New York, their friendship was all over. The next thing was that notice in the paper.

The Kid's idea was to go right down and wreck the Temple of the Inner Star, windin' up by havin' Honest Dan and his bunk medium pinched. I showed him where it would do no good, because he had set 'em up in business and if they was crooked the jury would figure that and put the Kid's name on one of them indictments. He calmed off finally and said he'd be satisfied to let it go at half killin' 'em both and makin' a bum out of the Temple of the Inner Star.

We got down there in a few minutes, and Honest Dan meets us at the door. He's all excited and says the time has come for the big hog killin', after which they're gonna blow New York, because they been tipped off that the new police commissioner is about to startle the natives with a raid. The Kid starts to bawl him out, when the big stout dame is ushered into the room and Dan hustles us into the professor's shrine in the rear.

As soon as she gets inside, the professor tells her to prepare for a shock. She shivers all over, grabbin' the side of the chair and takin' a long whiff out of a little green bottle. Then she says she'll try and be brave, and to let her have the works. The professor says he has finally dug up Marc Anthony, and all the spirits is in there tryin' for them, so's they can be brought together. He told her to go right back to her rooms at the Fitz-Charlton and he would send out the old thought waves for Marc. Just when he'd get him, he didn't know—it might be a day, a week or a month, but she was to sit there all dolled up to receive him and wait. He said she would know Marc, because he would have a snake tattooed on the third finger of his right hand in memory of the way Cleopatra kissed off. That's all he was allowed to give out just now, he winds up.

Well, the stout dame thanks him about six hundred times and waddles out darn near hysterical. She grabs hold of her daughter and hisses in her ear,

"Oh, Gladys, they've found him! My beloved Marc Anthony is coming to claim me for his own. Then we will return to Egypt, and, sitting upon a golden throne—"

Friend daughter pulls a weary smile and leads Cleopatra to the door.

"Oh, don't, mother!" she says. "Don't! If you only knew how all this sickens me! This man has hypnotized you! Why don't you listen to me and take that trip to California where—"

"What!" squeals the stout dame. "What? Be away when my Marc comes? How dare you think of such a thing! I did that once and if you have read your ancient history, you must remember the terrible result!"

Daughter sighs, shakes her head and they go out.

Now the Kid has been takin' all this stuff in without lettin' a peep out of him and when the stout dame has left, I figured he'd tear right in to the plotters, so I got ready to hold up my end and reached for a chair. But what d'ye think the Kid did? He falls down on a sofa and starts to laugh! On the level, I bet he snickered out loud for a good fifteen minutes and then he gets up and walks to the door without sayin' a single word to either Dan or the professor, after all that stuff he pulled on me at the hotel!

While we're goin' down in the elevator, Honest Dan tells us that they got a handsome actor who just now is playin' in a show called "Standin' on the Corners, Waitin' for a Job," and they're gonna have him get a snake painted on the third finger of his right hand and shoo him up to the stout dame the next day. After he has been welcome homed, Marc Anthony is gonna say that he's makin' out a check for the professor which throwed them together, and don't she think she ought to send in somethin' also? When she asks what he thinks would be about right, Marc Anthony is gonna say that he guesses she ought to keep the pen she wrote the check with as a souvenir, but that everything else she had, includin' anything a pawnbroker would give a ticket on, would do!

I didn't say nothin' to that, but I was doin' a piece of thinkin' and as soon as we got our feet on Fifth Avenue again, I let go. I told the Kid what I thought of his friend Honest Dan in language that Billy Sunday could have been proud of. When I got through with Dan, I took up the professor and give him a play. I said it was my belief that a couple of safety-first crooks, who would deliberate trim a simple old stout dame out of her dough in that coarse manner, should be taken up to the Metropolitan tower and eased off.

The Kid just grins and starts hummin' under his breath.

By this time I had worked myself up to such a pitch that my goat was chasin' madly about the streets, and to have the Kid act that way was about all I needed. I carefully explained to him just how many kinds of a big, yellah tramp he was, to let the professor crab him with Miss Vincent and get away with it clean. I showed him where he should have at least bent a chair over that guy's head, if he was a real gentleman whose honor had been trifled with and not a four flushin' false alarm.

"Gobs of generous Gazoopis!" he snickers at me when I get through. "Our employees is all new, noisy and Norwegians!"

They was a queer look in his eye, and I figured he must have slipped out in the mornin' at that and dug up a place where prohibition hadn't carried. I stopped right in the middle of the traffic and told him I was goin' up to the Fritz-Charlton the next mornin' and tip the stout dame off, if it was the last thing I did.

He just grins!

The next mornin' I beat it up to Cleopatra's hotel, and, after I have waited an hour, she sends a maid down to see me.

The maid tells me to spread my hands out flat on a little table that's standin' there and she examines every finger like a sure enough mechanic looks over a second-hand automobile he's gonna buy to hack with. Finally, she throws my hands down with a disappointed look and her shoulders begins one of them hula dances.

"*Viola*!" she remarks. "That leetle snake, he is not there! Madame she is not at home—away wit' you!"

Well, I figures I did what *I* could, so I breezed out and left Cleopatra flat.

Failin' to locate the Kid anywheres, I went on down to the studio and walk right in on the professor and Honest Dan givin' Marc Anthony a dress rehearsal. He was a handsome guy, all right, sickenin'ly so, with one of them soft, mushy faces and wavin' blonde hair. He's had the snake tattooed on his finger, like the part called for, and the way he carries on about how he's gonna give the stout dame the work makes me foam at the mouth. My once favorably known left had all it could do to keep from bouncin' off his chin! Finally, they start him away and Honest Dan tells me how they got it framed up for him to meet Cleopatra. He was to go to the Fritz-Charlton and send up a card that claimed he was the editor of "Society Seethings," and when she comes down to see him, he was to ask her what was her plans for the winter season and a lot of bunk like that. In no way was he to make a crack about bein' Marc Anthony—that would be too raw, but as he was leavin' he was to carelessly let her see that snake on his finger. That was all!

They knowed Cleopatra would do the rest.

I couldn't stand no more, so I hustled back to our hotel, and the minute I get in, the clerk tells me the Kid has been chasin' around lookin' for me all morning so I beat it right up to our suite. The Kid is doin' his road work by canterin' around the room when I come in, and he rushes over and grabs me by the arm.

"When are them yeggmen gonna send Marc Anthony up to Cleopatra?" he demands, all excited.

"He just left a few minutes ago!" I tells him. "Why?"

The Kid gives a yell and jumps over to the door leadin' to our sittin'-room, yankin' it open with one jerk. I thought I'd pass away when I got a flash at what was inside. They was about twenty of the roughest lookin' guys I ever seen in my life, all dolled up in new suits, shoes and hats. Some of them I recognized as ex-heavy-weights, they was a few strikin' longshoremen, a fair sprinklin' of East Side gunmen and here and there what had passed for a actor in the tanks.

"Some layout, eh?" pipes the Kid, rubbin' his hands together. "It took me all mornin' and nearly three hundred bucks to rib them guys up, but they're all desperate, darin' and dolled up!"

"What the—what's the big idea?" I gasps.

"Hold up your hands!" roars the Kid at his rough and readys.

They did—and I got it!

Each and every one of them guys had a snake tattooed on the third finger of his right hand!

The Kid had probably put in the mornin' rehearsin' 'em, because all he had to say now was, "Go to it!" and they beat it. He told me they was all goin' up to the Fritz-Charlton and ask for the stout dame at three minute intervals, show their right hand and claim they was Marc Anthony!

"If that don't show the stout dame that the professor is the bunk and if she don't let out a moan that'll be plainly heard at police headquarters, I'll make Dan a present of the five thousand he took me for!" says the Kid.

In about a hour the telephone begins to ring and I answers it. When the ravin' maniac on the other end of the wire got to where he could control the English language, I found out it was no less than Honest Dan. The main thing he said was for us to come down to the Temple of the Inner Star right away, because him and the professor has got in a terrible jam. We hopped in a taxi and did like he said. Honest Dan is waitin' in the elevator for us, and he looked like the loser in a battle royal. He says the stout dame has just left, and she's in a terrible state. I could believe that easy, because they is nothin' more vicious in the land of the free than a enraged come-on. I'd rather face a nervous wildcat than face a angry boob!

"Somebody put the bee on us!" howls Honest Dan, wringin' his hands. "And a truckload of guys went up to the hotel claimin' they was Marc Anthony in voices that disturbed people in China. They throwed the real Marc out on his lily white ear, and seven of 'em got pinched for disorderly conduct. I understand they was a mêlée up there that would make a football game look like chess and the papers is havin' a field day with the thing! We got to grab Cleopatra's gems and go away from here before the whole plant is uncovered."

"Why," I says, "how are you gonna take the stout dame now? She knows it's a fake, don't she?"

"Fake, hell!" hollers Dan. "*She thinks it's on the level*! The only thing that bothers her is which one is the *right* Marc Anthony. She says two of them had such patrician faces that she thinks some of the Caesars has got mixed up with the lot. She's gonna put it up to her late husband, and she's comin' back here any minute to talk with his spirit!" He begins walkin' the floor. "I never seen no dame like that!" he busts out. "She *wants* to be trimmed! The only thing she seemed to be sore about was the fact that she couldn't pick out the right Marc Anthony. Now we git the chance of a lifetime to grab a roll when she comes back and we ain't got no ghost! If I could only get the guy that sent all them Marc Anthonys up there," he winds up with a yell, "I'd make a ghost out of him!"

He never seemed to think the Kid might have done it, because the Kid was the boy that had set him and the professor up in business and why should he crab his own play?

A little electric buzzer makes good while Honest Dan is ravin' away, and Dan, gettin' white, grabs the Kid by the arm and begs him to come to the rescue.

"Jump in that cabinet there!" he whispers to him. "And when this dame asks if you're Henry, say yes, and tell her the real Marc Anthony is the guy with the blonde hair, and he's now at the City Hospital. That's all you got to say and—"

He shoves the Kid back of the cabinet and me back of a curtain just as Cleopatra blows in with her daughter. Honest Dan tells them to be seated quick, because the professor has just got the spirit of her husband where he's ready to talk to the reporters. The West Indian hall boys sneak around in the back, rattlin' chains and bangin' on pans. Then Dan reaches back and opens the mechanical bellows, and a blast of cold air comes into the room while a white light flashes over the cabinet.

"Now!" whispers Dan to the stout dame, "speak quick!"

At that minute, Dan looked like a guy with a ticket on a hundred to one shot, watchin' it breeze into the stretch leadin' by by a city block.

"Is—is that you Henery?" squeaks Cleopatra in a tremblin' voice.

They's a rustle in the cabinet and then *this* comes out over the top.

"Generous gobs of Gazoopis! Our employees is ready, reckless and Russian. This guy is crooked, crazy and careless. He will take you for your beautiful, bulgin' bankroll and—"

"Why, Henery!" squawks the dame, jumpin' up off the chair.

I heard the well known dull thud on the other side of the cabinet, and I guess it was Professor Parducci fallin' senseless on the floor. I thought Honest Dan had dropped dead from the way he was hung over a sofa.

"Each and every day," goes on the voice in the cabinet,

"each and every day we ship a million lovely loaves—"

"Merciful Heavens!" yells the dame. "A sign! Henery, shall I go back?"

"Back is right!" says the voice. "These guys is cheap crooks and they ain't no Marc Anthony!"

The lights go out and Honest Dan comes to, rushin' over to the stout dame with a million alibis tryin' to be first out of his mouth. I beat it around to the back, but the professor has gone somewheres else while the goin' was fair to medium.

"You have deceived me, you wretch!" screams the stout dame. "You have—"

That's as far as she got, because right in the middle of it she pulls a faint, and daughter eases her to the floor. The Kid hops out of the cabinet and grabs Honest Dan.

"Beat it, you rat," bawls Scanlan, "before I commit mayhem!"

From the way Honest Dan went out of that room, he must have passed Samoa, the first hour!

Daughter reaches up and grabs the Kid's hand.

"I—I—want to thank you," she says, "for saving my mother. I—I don't know what might have happened, if you hadn't been here!"

"That's all right!" pipes the Kid. "D'ye want us to do anything else?"

"Yes," she says. "Will you tell me where you heard that— that description of the—the million lovely loaves?"

"Sure," answers the Kid. "When we was comin' East, we stopped off at a hick burg somewheres and a guy took us over a bakery—"

Daughter claps her hands and laughs.

"Poetic justice!" she says. "That explains everything. My poor, dear father founded that bakery, and those were the last advertisements for it he wrote!"

CHAPTER VII
LIFE IS REEL!

The nation is bein' flooded these days with advertisements claimin' that any white man which works for less than forty thousand bucks a year is a sucker. The best of 'em is wrote by a friend of mine, Joe Higgins, who gets all of twenty bucks every Saturday at six—one-thirty in July, August and September.

The ads that Joe tears off deals with inventions. He shows that Edison prob'ly wouldn't of made a nickel over a million, if he hadn't discovered everything but America, and that Bell, Marconi, Fulton and that gang, wouldn't of been any better known to-day than ham and eggs, if they hadn't used their brains for purposes of thinkin' and invented somethin'. There's fortunes which would make the Vanderbilts and Astors look like public charges, explains Joe, awaitin' the bird which will quit playin' Kelly pool some night and invent a new way to do *anything*.

The ad winds up with the important information that the people which Joe works for is so close to the patent office gang that they could get French fried potatoes copyrighted. For the sum of "write for particulars," they'll rush madly from Washington papers that'll protect any idea you got, before some snake-in-the-grass friend plies you with strawberry sundaes and steals your secret. At the bottom of this there's a long list of things sadly needed by a sufferin' public, which will willin'ly shower their inventor with medals and money,—things like non-playable ukaleles, doctors which can guess what's the matter with *you* instead of your bankroll, grape fruit that won't hit back while you're eatin' it, non-refillable jails and so forth. All you got to do is stake yourself to a couple of test tubes, a white apron and a laboratory, hire Edison, Marconi, Maxim and Hennery Ford as assistants—with the U. S. Mint in back of you in case expenses come up—and you'll wake up some mornin' to find yourself the talk of Fall River.

I been lookin' over these ads for a long time, but there's three names I never seen on the list of famous inventors. They are to wit: the guy that discovered the only absolute cure for rheumatism, the one that invented the dope book on the female race and the bird that holds a patent on the complete understandin' of human nature. I guess the reason I never seen *their* names is because the thing ain't really been decided yet— there seems to be some difference of opinion. But if you wanna find out how many guys there are that swear they invented *all* them things, look up the population of the world. The figures is exactly the same.

I ain't met nobody yet which didn't admit they had the only correct dope on women, rheumatism and human nature, but I'm still waitin' to be introduced to the guy which really knows anything at all about *any* of 'em, when it gets right down to the box score!

The nearest I ever come to knowin' the original patentee to two of 'em was Eddie Duke. Eddie is one of the best men in the movable picture game, accordin' to everybody but himself. *He* concedes he's *the* best. He's a little, aggressive guy which would of prob'ly been a lightweight champion, for instance, if it hadn't been for his parents. They killed off his chances of makin' *big* money, by slippin' him a medium dose of education when he was too young to fight back. Eddie's like a million other guys I know, all Half-way Henrys, you might call 'em. Too much brains to dig streets and not enough to own 'em! Unhappy mediums that always calls *somebody* boss!

We're sittin' in Duke's office one mornin', when without even knockin'—a remarkable thing for a movie star—in walks Edmund De Vronde. Edmund has caused more salesladies to take their pens in hand than any other actor in the world. His boudoir is hung with pictures of dames from eight to eighty and from Flatbush to Florida. If some of 'em was actual reproductions, them dames was foolish for sellin' shirtwaists, believe me! Edmund is as beautiful as five hundred a week and built like Jack Dempsey. Off the screen he's as rough and ready as a chorus man.

"Hello, Cutey!" says the Kid, who liked De Vronde and carbolic acid the same way.

"I've come to ask a favor," says De Vronde.

"Well," Duke tells him, lightin' a cigarette and lookin' straight at the end of it, "we ain't gonna pay for no more autographed photos, we won't fire the press agent, you gotta finish this picture with Miss Hart and both them camera men that's shootin' this movie is high-class mechanics and stays! Outside of that, I'm open to reason."

"What I want will cost you nothing," says De Vronde. "That is—practically nothing. My dresser,—the silly idiot!— tendered me his resignation this morning!"

"Well, what's all this gotta do with me?" he asks De Vronde. "I can't be bothered diggin' up valets to see that you got plenty of fresh vanilla cold cream every morning and that they's ample talcum powder on the chiffonier! I got—"

"I have already secured a man," interrupts De Vronde. "He happens to be a—a—friend of mine. The poor fellow is desperately in need of work. He's in Denver at present, and I'd like to have him on as soon as possible. If we're to begin that big feature on Monday, I'm sure I can't be bothered thinking about where this shirt and that cravat is, and just what color combinations will be best for my costume in the gypsy cave."

"That's right!" grins the Kid. "Figure for yourself what would happen, if Cutey forgot his mustache curler, for instance. The whole country would be, now, aghast, and he'd be a nervous wreck in five minutes!"

"So if you'll kindly telegraph the fare to this address," goes on De Vronde, ignorin' the Kid, "I'll be obliged."

With that he blows.

"And the tough part of it is," moans Duke, reachin' for a 'phone, "I'll have to do just that! It'll cost about sixty bucks to import this bird here and when he gets here, it's nothin' but another mouth to feed. If I had half the nerve of that big stiff De Vronde, I'd take a German quartette over to London and make 'em sing the 'Wacht Am Rhein' in front of Buckin'ham Palace!"

"He claims this valet's a friend of his, too," says the Kid. "I'll bet he'll turn out to be another one of them sweet spirits of nitre boys, eh?"

"If he is," growls Duke, "it won't be two days before he'll be sick and tired of the movie game, you can bet two green certificates on that!"

A week later, me and the Kid is standin' near the entrance to Film City talkin' to Miss Vincent, when a young feller blows in through the gates and walks up to us. He's one of them tall birds, as thin as a dime, and his clothes has been brushed right into the grain. When the light hit him, I seen they was places where even the grain had quit. His shoes is so run over at the heels that they'd of fit nice and snug into a car track and he'd just gone and shaved himself raw.

One good look and this bird checked up as a member in good standin' of one of the oldest lodges in the world. They got a branch in every city, and they was organized around the time that Adam and Eve quit the Garden of Eden for a steam-heated flat. The name of this order is "The Shabby Genteels."

But what transfixed the eye and held the attention, as we remark in the workhouse, was this guy's face. I might say he had the most inconsistent set of features I ever seen off the screen. He ain't a thousand miles from bein' good-looking and his chin is well cut and square, like at one time he'd been willin' to hustle for his wants and fight for 'em once he got 'em, but that time ain't *now*! His eyes is the tip-off. They don't look straight into yours when he talks—the liar's best bet!—or they don't look at the ground, but they stare off over your shoulder into the air, like he's seein' somethin' *you* can't, and it ain't pleasant to look at.

I've seen that look on beaten fighters, when the winner is settin' himself for the knockout, and I've seen it on the faces of other guys, when some smug-jowled judge has reached into their lives and took ten or twenty years as a deposit on what they'll do with the rest. It's a look you don't forget right away, take it from me!

Well, this feller that's walkin' up to us had that look. If a director had yelled "Register despair!" at him, he could of just looked natural and they'd of thought he was another Mansfield.

And he's *young*! Get that?

"Pardon me!" he says, takin' off his hat. "Where can I find Mister De Vronde?"

The Kid puts his hand on his arm and swings him around, "You'll pro'bly find him over behind the Street Scene in Venice," he tells him. "If he ain't there, look around the Sahara Desert for him—know him when you see him?"

The other guy looks at us for a minute like he thinks he's bein' kidded. Then he pulls a slow, tired grin.

"I think so," he says. "Thanks!"

When he walks away, I turns to Miss Vincent.

"That's prob'ly Cutey De Vronde's new guardeen," I says. "I guess he—"

"You and the Kaiser is the same kind of guessers!" butts in the Kid. "He guessed we wouldn't scrap! If that guy we was just talkin' to is a lady's maid for Cutey, I can sing like Caruso!"

"He doesn't look like a valet," says Miss Vincent, kinda doubtful.

"I don't blame him!" says the Kid. "And lemme tell you, he never got them muscles from brushin' clothes and buttonin' vests. I felt his arm when I swung him around that time, and this guy is just about as soft as the Rock of Gibraltar!"

"I can't understand," says Miss Vincent, "how a strong,

healthy man can be a valet—ugh!" she winds up, with a little shiver.

"That's easy," sneers the Kid. "A *man* can't!"

Well, a man *did*! Gimme your ears, as the deaf guy said.

The next mornin' it turns out that I can guess like a rabbit can run. The new entry on the payroll borrehs a match from me, and durin' the tête-à-tête that folleyed, I find out that his name is John R. Adams and, as far as the world in general and America in particular is concerned, it could of been George Q. Mud. Durin' the lifetime of twenty-nine years he's been on earth, he's tried his hand at everything from bankin' to bartenderin', and so far the only thing he's been a success at is bein' a failure. At that he leads the league. And now, to top it all off, he's a valet for a movie hero!

"It's all a matter of luck!" he says, bitterly. "A man who tries these days is not an ambitious hustler, but a *pest* to the powers above him! I defy a man to stand on his own feet and make good without influence. It's not *what* do you know any more, but *who* do you know! I've been a bookkeeper, a printer, a salesman, a chauffeur, a bank clerk, and, yes, even a chorus man. At every one of those things I gave the best I had in stock to get to the front. Did I get there? Not quite!" he throws away the cigarette he's hardly had a puff of. "Why?" he asks me. "Because in every trade or profession there's somebody with half the sand and ability, who don't know the job's requirements but knows the boss's son! I'm not a quitter or I wouldn't be here, but I'm sick and disgusted with this thing called life and—"

"And that's why you never got nowhere!" breaks in a voice behind us—and there's Eddie Duke. Adams flushes up and starts away, but Eddie pulls him back.

"Listen to me, young feller!" he says. "I happened to hear your moan just now and your dope is all wrong. There ain't no such thing as luck; if there was, a blacksmith is the luckiest guy in the world and oughta make a million a minute, because he's handlin' nothin' but horseshoes all day long, ain't he? Forget about that luck stuff! Makin' good is all in the way you look at it, anyways. A bricklayer makin' thirty bucks a week, raisin' a family and bringin' home his pay every Saturday night in his pocket instead of on his breath, is makin' good as big as J. P. Morgan is—d'ye get me? Yes, sir, that bird can say he's got over! Makin' good is like religion, every other guy has a different idea of what it means, but there's many a feller swingin' a pick that's makin' good just as much as the bird that owns the ditch—in his own way! You claim a guy's got to know somebody these days to get over, eh? Well, you got that one right, I'll admit it!"

"Of course!" says Adams, brightenin' up. "That's my argument and—"

"That ain't no argument, that's a whine!" sneers Duke, cuttin' him off short. "Listen to me—you bet you gotta know somebody to get anywheres, *you gotta know yourself*! That's all! Just lay off thinkin' how lucky the other guy is, and give Stephen X. You a minute's attention. You may be the biggest guy in the world at *somethin'*, if you'll only check up on yourself and see what that somethin' is! Remember Whosthis says, 'Full many a rose is born to blush unseen—' Well, don't be one of them desert flowers; come into the city and let 'em all watch you blush. Get me? How did you happen to meet this big stiff De Vronde?"

Adams gets pale for a second and clears his throat.

"I'm working for him," he says slowly, like he's thinkin' over each word before lettin' it go, "and I don't care to discuss him."

At just that minute, De Vronde, Miss Vincent, the Kid and another dame come rollin' up in Miss Vincent's twelve-cylinder garage-mechanic's friend. De Vronde hops out and walks over to us, wavin' his cane and frownin'.

"Look here!" he bawls at Adams. "I thought I told you to be at the east gate with my duster and goggles? You've kept me waiting half an hour, while you're gossiping around! Really, if you're going to start this way, I shall have to get another man. Look sharp now, no excuses!"

The Kid winks at me, noddin' to Adams who's lookin' at De Vronde with a very peculiar gaze. I couldn't quite get what he's registerin'. Miss Vincent looks interested and sits up. The other dame opens the door of the car and stands on the runnin' board.

"Here's where the fair Edmund gets his and gets it good!" hisses Duke in my ear, lookin' at Adams.

"I'm very sorry," says Adams, suddenly. "I should have remembered."

And without another word or look, he exits.

"Yellah!" snorts the Kid.

"No spine!" sneers Miss Vincent.

"Nick-looking boy—who is he?" asks the other dame, lookin' after him.

Duke slaps his hands together all of a sudden and gazes at her like a guy gettin' his first flash at his hour-old son. Then he looks after Adams, grins and claps his hands again.

"Who is he?" repeats the dame.

De Vronde sneers.

"Really," he says, "your interest is surprising. That fellow is my—"

"Shut up!" roars Duke, springin' to the runnin'-board. "Here!" he goes on, talkin' fast. "I'm gonna shoot them two interiors in half a hour, so you better call this joy ride off!" He turns to the strange dame and speaks very polite, "Miss Vincent will show you everything; if you want anything, just 'phone the office."

When they're gone, Duke turns to me and grins.

"I often heard you say you made Scanlan welterweight champ," he says, "by *pickin'* the guys he was to fight till he got where he could lick 'em *all*. Well, I'm gonna do the same thing for our friend Mister Jack Adams, valet for Edmund De Vronde, the salesladies' joy. I'm goin' in that boy's corner from this day on, and, when I get through, he'll be a champ!"

"What?" I says. "Train a guy like that for the ring? Why —"

"I see you don't make me," he interrupts, "which is just as well, because you'd be liable to ball the whole thing up, if you did. This kid Adams has got symptoms of bein' a he-man in his face. He's hit the bumps good and hard and right now he's down, takin' a long count. Now whether he needs to be helped or kicked to his feet, I don't know, but I'm the baby that's gonna stand him up!"

"Well," I tells him, "go to it! But the thing I can't figure, is what d'you care if he gets over or not—who pays *you* off on it?"

He looks me over for a minute, registerin' deep thought.

"I'm gonna give you the works!" he says finally. "And if you ever mention a word of this to anybody, they'll have to identify your body afterwards by that green vest you got!"

"Rockefeller's three dollars short of havin' enough money to make me tell!" I says.

"Fair enough!" says Duke. "Did you notice that strange dame which was with Miss Vincent in the car just now?"

"The blonde that would of made Marc Anthony throw away Cleopatra's 'phone number?" I asks. "Yeh—I noticed her. Easily that!"

"Well," he says, "this dame, which was such a knockout to you, is Miss Dorothy Devine. When her father died last year, she become a orphan."

"Well, that's tough," I says. "Me and the Kid will kick in with any amount in reason and—"

"Halt!" said Eddie. "Her dear old father only left her a pittance of fifty thousand a year and two-thirds control of the company we're all workin' for out here. Now besides bein' several jumps ahead of the average dame in looks, Dorothy is a few centuries ahead of the movies in ideas. She claims we're all wrong, and she's gonna revolutionize the watch-'em-move photo industry. That's what she's here for now!"

"Well," I says after a bit, "what d'ye expect *me* to do— bust out cryin'?"

"Not yet!" he says. "I'll tell you when. Accordin' to Dorothy, all the pictures we put out are rotten. Our heroes and villains are plucked alive from dime novels and is everything but true to life. Our heroines belong in fairy tales and oughta be let stay there. *She* claims that no beautiful girl with more money than the U. S. Mint would fall for the handsome lumberjack, and that no guy who couldn't do nothin' better than punch cows would become boss of the ranch through love of the owner's daughter. All that stuff's the bunk, she says. Her dope is that a real man would boost himself to the top, girl or no girl, and the woman never lived which could put a man over, if he didn't have the pep himself. As a finish, she tells me that no healthy, intelligent girl would stand for the typical movie hero. A bird which would go out and ride roughshod over all the villains like they do in the films would nauseate her, she says, and we have no right to encourage this bunk by feedin' it to an innocent public!"

"Eddie," I says, "she ain't a mile off the track, at that! This—"

"Oh, she ain't, eh?" he snarls. "Well that shows that you and her knows as much about human nature as I do about makin' a watch! Miss Devine wants us to put on a movie that she committed herself, and, if we do, we'll be the laughin' stock of the world and Big Bend. It's got everything in it but a hero, a heroine, a villain, action and love interest. It's about as hot as one of them educational thrillers like 'Natives Makin' Panama Hats in Peoria' would be. A couple of these would put the company on the blink, and I lose a ten-year contract at ample money a year!"

"Well," I says, "what are you gonna do—quit?"

"Your mind must be as clean as a baby's," he says, "because you got your first time to use it! No, I ain't gonna quit! I'm gonna show Miss Dorothy Devine that as a judge of movin' pictures, she's a swell-lookin' girl. I like these tough games, a guy feels so good all over when he wins 'em. She's startin' with all the cards—money, looks and, what counts more, she's just about the Big Boss here now. All I got is one good card and that's only a jack—Jack Adams, to be exact—and I'm gonna beat her with him!"

"I'll fall!" I says. "How?"

"Well," he tells me, "my argument is that all these thrillers we put on are sad, weary and slow compared to some of the things that happen in real life every day that we never hear about. They's many a telephone girl, for instance, makin' a man outa a millionaire's no-good son and many a sure-enough heiress bein' responsible for the first mate on a whaler becomin' her kind and a director in the firm! I claim it does *good* and not harm, to feed this stuff to a trustin' public by way of the screen. Why? Because every shippin'-clerk that's sittin' out in front puts himself in the hero's place and every salesgirl dreams that she's the heroine. Without thinkin', they both get to pickin' up the virtues we pin on our stars, and it can't *help* but do 'em good! I don't know who started the shimmy, but I know women and I know human nature, and knowin' 'em both, I'm gonna make a sportin' proposition to Miss Dorothy Devine!"

"What's the bet?" I says. "I may take some of it myself."

"The bet is this," he tells me. "Here's this boy Adams, who, bein' De Vronde's valet, is undisputed low man in Film City. He's disgusted with life, he ain't got the ambition of a sleepin' alligator, or nerve enough to speak harshly to *himself*. All right! If Miss Devine will follow my orders for a couple of weeks without Adams knowin' who or what she is, I claim that bird will make good! All that guy needs is a reason for tryin', and she can make herself it!"

"You don't expect a dame like that to make love to a guy that cleans De Vronde's shoes, do you?" I asks him.

"You must of been a terrible trial to teacher when you went to school!" he snorts. "No!—I don't want her to make love to him. I want to prove to her that the things we put in the movies is happenin' all the time in real life, only more so! I want her to make Adams *feel* just how far back he's gone. I want her to cut him dead, because he's a valet, and let him know that's the reason. Then nature and him will do the rest, or I'll pay off! Who put Adam over? Eve! All right, I'm gonna wind this thing up and let it go. I'll take the best scenes from the last six pictures we put out, and make Adams and Miss Devine play 'em out, without either of 'em knowin' it. They oughta be a villain, and I'm shy one just now, but I'll lay six to five that one will turn up!"

"Look here!" I says. "Suppose Miss Devine should fall for this Adams guy for *real*! Did you ever figure that?"

"Yes!" he snorts. "And suppose the Pacific Ocean is made outa root beer!"

I guess Miss Devine must of been a sport, because Duke starts his stunts off the next day. She promised to give Adams a month to show signs of life and to do exactly as Duke tells her. Adams ain't to be told a thing about it, and Miss Devine giggles herself sick over how she's gonna show Duke the difference between real life and the movies. They put up a thousand bucks apiece.

The first action come off when Miss Devine and Adams meets in the "Sahara Desert" set.

"Good morning!" pipes Adams, bowin' and raisin' his hat.

"I beg your pardon!" comes back Miss. Devine, drawin' herself up and presentin' him with a glance that's colder than a dollar's worth of ice.

"I—I—said good morning!" stammers Adams, kinda flustered.

"You have made a mistake, my man!" she says, each word bein' about twenty below zero. "A mistake I shall report to your master. I—"

"But—," begins Adams, gettin' red. "You—"

"That will do!" she cuts him off. "I'm not in the habit of arguing with servants. You may go!"

Sweet cookie!

The poor kid looks like he'd stopped one with his chin and for the first time since I'd seen him, he straightens up with his hard, white face fairly quiverin'. I thought he was ready for a peach of a come-back, but he fooled me. He walks off without a word.

Miss Devine laughs like a kid with a new rattle and snaps her fingers after him.

The next day, Duke is directin' a scene in a big thriller they're puttin' on and Miss Devine is appearin' in it as a super at his orders. She's wearin' enough jewels to free Ireland and she looked better than 1912 would look to Germany. Adams is standin' on one side with his arms full of De Vronde's different changes.

Duke looks at Miss Devine for a minute and then raises his voice.

"Say—you!" he bawls at her. "What's the matter, can't you hear? You made that exit wrong four times runnin', d'ye think we get this film for nothin'? What d'ye mean by comin' here and ruinin' this scene on me, eh? You wanna be a movie star, they tell me—well, you got the same chance that I have of bein' made Sultan of Turkey! If you can act, I'm King of Shantung! Why—"

Miss Devine gasps and looks more than ever like a rose, by turnin' a deep and becomin' shade of red. Nobody pays any attention to the thing. They'd all heard it a million times before, when Duke was rehearsin' supers.

Nobody but Adams!

He drops all of De Vronde's clothes right on the floor, and I thought the fair Edmund would faint away dead! Adams walks right through the camera men up to Duke and swings him around while he's still bawlin' out Miss Devine.

"That's enough!" he snarls, white to the ears. "One more word to this lady, and I'll knock you down! You hound—you wouldn't dare use that language to a man!"

Duke's eyes sparkle, but he looks Adams over coolly and sneers.

"Curse you, Jack Dalton!" he says. "Unhand that woman, or you shall feel my power, eh?" He sticks his chin close to Adams's face. "Take the air!" he growls. "Where d'ye get that leadin' man stuff? If I see you around here any more this afternoon, I'll fire you and you'll walk home for all the money you'll draw from this man's firm. Now, beat it!"

Adams hesitates a minute, and then he looks like on second thought he's scared at what he's done. He mumbles somethin' and walks right outa the picture, nor even turnin' when De Vronde squawks at him for walkin' over his silk duster which he'd throwed on the floor.

"That's all for now, ladies and gentlemen!" pipes Duke suddenly, turnin' to the bunch. "I'll shoot the rest of this to-morrow."

They all blow out except Miss Devine. Duke looks at her, rubbin' his hands together and grinnin'.

"All right!" she smiles back. "First honors! What will I do next?"

She didn't have to do nothin' next! The thing that Duke had started got away from him and Adams led all the tricks from then to the finish. Duke told me afterwards he felt like a guy which has lit a match on Lower Broadway and seen the Woolworth Buildin' go up in flames!

The very next afternoon, Mister Jack Adams becomes a star. Yes, sir!

A gang of supers is hangin' around the general offices waitin' for their pay. De Vronde and Miss Devine is sittin' at a cute little table under a tree drinkin' lemonade, and Adams is standin' with the supers, watchin'—Miss Devine.

"Look at that big stiff tryin' to make the dame!" pipes one of the extrys, a big husky grabbed up off the wharves in Frisco. He points at De Vronde. "If I was built like he is, I'd eat arsenic!"

Adams walks over to him.

"Why?" he says, very cool and hard.

"Heh?" says the super. "Why, look at 'im. Lookit the lace shirt he's wearin' and them pink socks. Why—"

"Shut up!" snarls Adams. "I know your kind—you think because a man bathes, shaves, speaks English and wears clean linen, that there's something wrong with him! You roughnecks resent the—"

"Well, I'd hate to be the family that brung that up!" interrupts the super. "Gawd! It makes a man sick to look at 'im!"

It all happened so quick that even Miss Devine and De Vronde didn't get it. They's just a sudden swish—a crack of bone meetin' bone, and the big super is flat on his ear! The rest of the gang mills around, shoutin' and yellin', and Adams prods the super with the toe of his shoe. I see Duke runnin' over with a couple of camera men which is so excited they've even brought their machines along.

"Listen!" spits out Adams, bendin' over the fallen gladiator. "Don't make any more remarks like that about—about Mister De Vronde, while I'm in this camp! If you do, I'll hammer you to mush! If you don't believe that, get up now and I'll illustrate it!"

The super plays dead, and Adams turns away.

By this time, Miss Devine and De Vronde, on the outskirts of the mob, has seen some of it.

"Really," says De Vronde, frowning "you'll have to stop

this brawling, Adams! I can't have my man—"

Adams gives him the up and down.

"Aw, shut up!" he snarls—and blows.

Well, right now I'm a million miles up in the air and no more interested in the thing than the bartenders was in final returns of the prohibition vote. They's two things I can't figure at all. One of 'em is why Adams should knock a man kickin' for roastin' De Vronde, who didn't have a friend in the place, and the other is what Duke and them camera men is doin' there.

About a week blows by, and then Miss Devine rides out alone one mornin' on a big white stallion. In a hour the horse trots into camp with the saddle empty. For the next twenty minutes they's more excitement in and about Film City than they was at the burnin' of Rome, but while Duke is gettin' up searchin' parties, Adams has cranked up Miss Devine's roadster and is a speck of dust goin' towards Frisco.

It was around five o'clock that afternoon, when he comes back and Miss Devine is sittin' beside him. Her ankle is all bound up with handkerchiefs and Adams is drivin' very slow and careful. He stops and then turns to help her outa the car, but she dodges his arm, steps down all by herself and without any sign of a limp, walks into the general offices.

Adams stands lookin' after her for a minute, kinda stunned.

"What was the matter?" I asks him, runnin' up.

"Why," he says, without lookin' at me; "she broke—she said she broke her ankle. She—"

Then he turns and runs the car into the garage.

The next mornin' he quits!

Duke broke the news, comin' over to Miss Devine, while I'm tellin' her how Kid Scanlan clouted his way up to the title.

"Well, Miss Devine," he growls, "I guess you win! Adams has left Film City flat on its back. I thought that bird had the stuff in him, but I guess you saw deeper than I did!"

"I guess I did!" says Miss Devine kinda slow. "I knew he'd never stay."

Duke clears his throat a coupla times, blows his nose and wipes his forehead with a silk handkerchief—his only dissipation.

"And now I got a confession to make," he says, throwin' back his shoulders like he's bracin' himself for a punch. "Ever since the day I played you against Adams, I been takin' a movie of you and him. Every time you was together they was a camera man—and a good one—in the offin'. You didn't know it and neither did Adams, but the result is a peach of a movie that'll make us a lot of money, if you'll let me release it. All I need is a couple more close-ups and—"

Miss Devine has been listenin' like she was in a trance. She turned more colors than they is in the flag, and, lemme tell you, they all become her!

"You—you—made a picture out of our—out of—me?" she gasps.

Whatever else Eddie Duke is, he's game.

"Yeh!" he nods. "And wait till you see it—it's great! Why, you got Pickford lookin' like a amateur, and Adams will be a riot with the girls the minute this movie's released! I wanted to prove to you that the movies ain't got a thing on real life, and I did! Why Adams can sign a contract with me any time he wants. That's makin' good, ain't it? From valet to movie star in five reels —and who put him over? *You*!!!"

Before Miss Devine can say anything, we hear voices behind us. We're standin' by a high hedge that had been set up for a picture that mornin', and it was Miss Devine that motioned us to keep quiet. The voices on the other side are Adams and De Vronde.

"I've done my share!" De Vronde is sayin'. "I've been sending home—"

"Eighty dollars a month!" cuts in Adams, in that new,

cold voice of his. "Eighty dollars a month to your father and mother, and you're making a thousand a week. Eighty dollars a month, and you pay a hundred and fifty for a suit! It's hard for me to call you a brother of mine! Do you know why I whipped that bum the other day? For what he said about you? No! Because I didn't want it thought that the whole family was as yellow as you are! But I'm going to make you game. You're going to turn what money you've hoarded over to Dad."

We're all lookin' at each other—dumb-founded! Even Duke is pale and pop-eyed.

"By the Eternal, Miss Devine," he whispers in her ear. "I swear I didn't know *that*! It don't happen in real life, eh? *Brothers*—by the dust of Methuselah!"

De Vronde is speakin', and we bend to listen.

"I can't!" he chokes out. "Why, I'll—"

We hear Adams snort.

"Stop!" he says. "You can make more money than I can and make Ma and Dad comfortable for the rest of their days. I'm going—"

"About that girl—that Miss Devine," De Vronde breaks in, his voice shaking "It's only right that you should know. She's made an ass of you—she and that Duke person! You've been followed about and everything you've done has been recorded by a camera. She had no accident the other day—her ankle wasn't hurt—the horse was sent back with the empty saddle deliberately—they photographed that, too! They had a silly bet of some sort and—"

Miss Devine steps deliberately right around the side of the hedge almost into Adams's arms. He's white and lookin' much like he did the first day he blowed into Film City. The minute he sees her he straightens up.

"How long have you been here?" he clips out.

"I've heard—everything!" she says, lookin' him right in the eye.

Adams runs his hand through his hair, and pulls a look that went through me to the bone. I don't know how it hit Miss Devine.

"And all of this—this—your attitude toward me—the accident—was played to make a picture?" he says.

"Yes!" says Miss Devine. "All except *this*!" And I hope I never see another movie, if both her arms didn't go around his neck—right out loud in public, too! "All except *this*!" she repeats. "And, oh, Jack—this is *real*!!"

"I win a thousand bucks!" pants Duke, draggin' me away —De Vronde blew the minute she appeared on the scene—"I win a thousand bucks!" he says. "And the picture is gonna be a riot! If they was only a good camera man here now for that close up at the finish, eh? Still—I guess that would be too raw!" He looks back where Adams and Miss Devine is posin' for a picture of still life. "And she said this love stuff was the bunk!" he hollers. "Oh, boy!!!!"

CHAPTER VIII
HOSPITAL STUFF

Every time I see a thermometer, a watch, and a egg my temperature aviates to about a hundred and ninety-eight in the shade—and if they's nobody lookin' I bust 'em! I spent two months and eight hundred bucks with that layout once and, oh, lady!—Say! The next time I feel a vacation comin' on, I'm goin' to Russia and holler, "Hooray for the Czar!"

I just been Red-Crossed to within a inch of my life and I'm off that "take-two-once-every-twice, and don't-eat-any-this-or-drink-any-that" stuff! The right cross and the double cross has been little pals of mine for years, and I once got throwed out of school for pullin' that "How to make a maltese cross" thing, but the *red* one was all new to me up to last month.

They call me a glutton for punishment, but I got—enough!

I can't go in a drug store no more, because the sight of the prescription bar in the rear affects me like strong drink and I even had to lay off peas, because they look like pills.

All the food I got durin' the time I become a victim of the Red Cross could have been carried over the Rocky Mountains by a lame ant, and I got a hole in my wrist that can be used as a ash tray from doctors grabbin' it to give my pulse early mornin' workouts and clockin' it over the full course. I was allowed two kinds of milk to drink—hot and cold. The only thing I could get to read was wrote to order on the premises and was all on the same subject, "Shake well before using!"

The whole thing was brought on by two words and Genaro, which was puttin' on this five-reel barbecue called "How Kid Scanlan Won the Title," and take it from me, if the Kid had pulled off in Manhattan some of the stunts he did in that picture, he would have won more than the welterweight title—he'd have won the oil business from Rockefeller the first night!

The two words was "Don't jump!" and Genaro *didn't* say

'em—if he had, the Kid would never have dove off a cliff and sprained his million-dollar left arm, which triflin' detail caused *me* to get my mail at a hospital for two months.

It was in the third reel of this picture, which I see by the billboards is liable to thrill the nation, that the thing happened. The Kid is supposed to jump off a cliff to fool the plotters which is tryin' to stop him from winnin' the title. They had picked out two of them cliffs—one of 'em was a drop of three feet and the other was a drop of twenty-one miles, accordin' to Scanlan, who made it and ought to know. Anyhow, it was far enough! They was gonna show a close-up of the high one first and then take a flash of Scanlan leapin' from the little one. The Kid walks to the edge of that high one, looks down and some fat-head camera man points a machine at him and starts turnin' the crank. Genaro was to wave his handkerchief as a signal for the Kid to dive off the *little* cliff and Scanlan, kinda puzzled, watches him. Just as he's walkin' away from the edge, Genaro blows his nose! The Kid sees the camera man and the handkerchief, and not wantin' to act yellah before the bunch, he—jumps!

A lot of excitement was had by all and Scanlan sprained his arm.

"Ah!" yells Genaro. "She'sa make the greata scene! What you think thisa Meester Scanlan he'sa joomp off wan mountain for art? That'sa real arteeste! He'sa killa himself for maka picture for Genaro! Ah—I embrace heem!"

Miss Vincent begins by faintin'. Then she comes to, throws a rock at a camera man which is takin' a close up of her unconscious, kneels at the Kid's side and kisses him right out loud before everybody. She claims, if he proves to be dead, she'll leave the company flat and have Genaro tried for murder before a judge which had been tryin' for two years to do somethin' for her. They finally carried the Kid up to the hotel, and sent for a doctor which was recommended by Eddie Duke. Accordin' to Eddie, this friend of his had the average doctor lookin' like a drug clerk. Pluckin' people from the grave was his specialty, says Eddie.

I guess they had to wait till this graverobber graduated from college, because it was over a hour before he showed up. He gets out of a buggy that was all the rage about the time Washington was thinkin' of goin' in the army, and the animal that was draggin' it along had been a total failure at tryin' to be a horse. The doc wasn't a day over seventy-five and he was dressed in a hat that must have come with the buggy, a pair of shoes like grandpa used to wear to work and a set of white whiskers. If he had any clothes on, I didn't see 'em. All I seen was them whiskers! I figured, if he had plucked people from the grave, like Eddie Duke claimed, he must have did it after they was dead.

He didn't look very encouragin' to me, but I led him upstairs and into the room where Scanlan was just comin' to and askin' what round it was. Eddie Duke and Miss Vincent was at his bedside, and the rest of the gang was outside the door arguyin' over which was the best undertaker in Frisco. I slipped away to a telephone booth and called up information.

"Gimme the best doctor in California!" I says, flickin' a jitney in the slot.

"For a nickel?" giggles the dame on the other end.

"Stop it!" I says. "I got a man here that's liable to croak any minute—this ain't no time for comedy! Ah—what time do you get off?"

"I never go out with strangers," she says, "but you got a nice voice at that. Where is your friend doin' his sufferin' at?"

"Film City!" I tells her. "And my voice ain't got nothin' on yours. I don't want to give you no short answer, but can I get the doctor now?"

"I got him waitin'," she says. "If I was you, I wouldn't let 'em fill your friend full of dope; fresh air and sunshine's got the druggist beat eighty ways! Good-by, Cutey—gimme a ring after the funeral!"

"This is the Hillcrest Sanitarium," pipes another voice over the wire, very sedate and dignified.

"And this is Johnny Green," I comes back, "manager of Kid Scanlan, the welterweight champ. We've throwed you people a lot of trade. Only a short while ago Scanlan flattened Young Hogan in two rounds, and Hogan was took there from the ring, remember? Well, I want the boss doctor there sent to Film City right away!"

With that begins a argument that went about fifteen minutes, and which I finally win by a shade. It seems it wasn't the regular thing for the head doctor there to answer night bells and so forth, like a ordinary medico, and the goin' was rather tough for awhile. Three or four times, when I was ready to quit, this telephone dame, which was takin' it all in with both ears, cut in with advice and helpful hints till the guy on the other end had enough and says he'll come.

The first thing that met my eye, when I got back to the Kid, was Eddie Duke's friend, the greatest doctor in the world. He was walkin' very fast away from the hotel and mutterin' to himself. I just had time to grab his arm, as he jumps in the buggy and reaches for the whip.

"Will he live, doc?" I asks him.

"Bah!" he snorts, jerkin' away from me. "The ignorant little pup!"

He whales Old Dobbin with the whip and leaves me flat.

I couldn't figure out what the Kid's education had to do with his health, so I beats it upstairs and all but fell over Eddie Duke. He's holdin' one eye and mumblin' somethin' about "roughnecks" and "ingratitude." I kept on through the crowd and into the Kid's room. Scanlan is still on the bed groanin', and beside him is the hotel clerk, thumbin' a almanac.

"Wait!" pants the clerk, as I come in. "I'll have it in a second." He turns over a lot more pages and then he hollers, "Ah! Here we are—what did I tell you? 'First Aid to the

Injured.'" He clears his throat and the Kid looks up hopefully. "Number one," reads the clerk. "'*First send for a physician!*'" He drops the book and dashes for the door. "Don't do nothing till I get back!" he yells.

Scanlan starts to go after him, but moans and falls back on the bed.

"I wish I had a gun!" he snarls. "That big boob has been here fifteen minutes tellin' me all he was gonna do for me as soon as he found it in the book! He—"

"Didn't the doctor do no good?" I butts in, sittin' on the side of the bed.

"Doctor?" says the Kid. "What doctor?"

"Eddie Duke's friend," I tells him. "The old—"

Scanlan leans up on his good arm.

"Listen, Johnny!" he says. "I still got a wallop in my right! Don't kid me now or—"

"What d'ye mean kid you?" I asks him. "Didn't the doctor—"

"Doctor!" he interrupts me, slammin' down the pillow. "If that guy was a doctor, I'm Caruso! He comes in here where I'm practically dyin' and tries to sell me a book!"

"Gimme it all!" I gasps.

"He sits down at the bed," explains the Kid, "and takes a big, black book out of what I figured was his medicine chest. He holds it up and asks me if I see it and I says I did, thinkin' I had passed the first test easy. Then he says he wrote the book himself and it's full of hope and cheer or dope and beer—to tell you the truth, I don't know which it was on account of the pain. Anyhow, I let him get away with it, and he tells me to think of how lucky I actually am alongside of the Crown's Prince of Germany—and then he begins to read from that book! It seems it's a novel about faith bein' stronger than pain. By this time, I seen that he was either nutty or tryin' to kid me, so I cut him off by askin' him when he's gonna fix up my arm. He says he's doin' it now, and when he gets through, he'll leave the book which will be a total of twenty-five bucks. When I come to, I ask him how long he had been a doctor, and he gets sore and claims he's a healer of the Mystic Sliders or somethin' like that, and what do I mean by callin' him a doctor? Then I called him a few other things so's he wouldn't have no kick comin' and gave him the bum's rush out of the room. Eddie Duke starts to moan about me maulin' his friend, and—well, get him to show you his eye!"

The door opens suddenly and Miss Vincent sticks the curls which all the shop girls is copyin' around the side of it.

"It's the doctor!" she whispers.

"Say!" pipes the Kid, grabbin' a pillow. "That old guy is game, eh?"

"A fightin' fool!" I agrees.

But this time a tall, solemn-lookin' guy breezes into the room and stares at me and the Kid with the same warm friendliness that a motorcycle cop regards a boob tryin' out a new auto. I figured he was the bird I had ordered by 'phone, and hit 1000 on the guess. He leans over the Kid, prods him around a bit, and then goes over him like he had lost somethin' and thought maybe he'd find it there. Then he straightens up and grunts.

"Hmph!" he says. "This man is a nervous wreck! Completely run down—needs rest and diet. I have my car outside and can take him over to the sanitarium, if—are you a relative?"

"His manager," I explains. "How about the arm, doc?"

"Nothing!" he says. "Wrenched—that's all. Come—help him downstairs, I'll wait."

I took out a five-case note.

"What do we owe you, doc?" I asks him, hopin' for the best.

"My consultation fee is fifty dollars!" he says, without battin' an eye.

I staggered back against the bureau.

"Every time you see me it's gonna set me back fifty?" asks the Kid, with tears in his voice.

The doc gives him a cold nod.

"Couldn't I take some treatment by mail?" pipes Scanlan, hopefully.

"Cease!" I says, takin' out the old checkbook. "What's your name, doc?"

"James," he says, "J. T. James."

"What's the J stand for?" I asks, shakin' out the pen.

"Jesse!" butts in Scanlan. "Heh, doc?"

"Do you mean to insinuate that I'm robbing you?" says the doc, frownin' at him.

"No," says the Kid, takin' the check from me and handin' it to him, "I don't blame a guy for tryin', but—"

I shut him off and dragged him downstairs before they was any hard feelin's. We climbed in the doctor's bus and at the Kid's request, Miss Vincent come along with us. Then we went after the road record between Film City and the Hillcrest Sanitarium. I guess this doctor was born with a steerin' wheel in his hand, because we took some corners on that trip that would have worried a snake, and when he threw her in high, we breezed along so swift we could have made a bullet quit. Finally, we come to a great big buildin' all hedged off with an iron fence and if you've ever seen a souvenir post card with "Havin' a fine time. Wish you were here," on it, you know what it looked like.

The doctor tells me and Miss Vincent to wait in the office, and he goes out with the Kid. In about fifteen minutes he's back and calls me over to a desk. They's a long piece of paper there and he says to sit down and fill it out, but, after one flash at it, I asked him could I take it home to work over, because my fountain pen was better on sprints than long distance writin' and this looked like a good two-hour job. He gives me another one of them North Pole stares and remarks that if the thing ain't filled out at once, the Kid won't be admitted to the sanitarium.

"He's in now, ain't he?" I comes back.

"Yes!" he snaps. "And he'll be out, if that paper isn't drawn up instantly!"

Miss Vincent giggles and hisses in my ear.

"They say the child is in London!" she pipes. "Sign that paper, curse you! We are in his power!"

Well, I seen I had to do a piece of writing so I grabbed up that paper and let the fountain pen go crazy. I give the Kid's entire name, where he was born, what his people did to fool the almshouse, what was his mother's maiden name and why, whether he went to church or Billy Sunday, was he white and could he prove it, who started the war and a lot of bunk like that. The guy who doped out the entrance examinations for that hospital must have been figurin' on how many he could keep *out*. When I run out of ink, I took out a copy of the *Sportin' Annual*, tore off the Kid's record and pasted it at the bottom of the page.

"How's that?" I asks, passin' it over.

"Very well," he says, glancin' at it. "Mister Scanlan is in room 45. That will be one-fifty—a hundred and fifty!"

"The price," I says, gettin' dizzy. "Not your weight!"

"That's the price," he tells me. "A hundred and fifty a week."

"I'm afraid the old bankroll is *too* weak," I says,—"too weak for that, anyhow. Drag the Kid out of that bridal suite and let him sleep in the hall. I'll—"

"Why, the idea!" butts in Miss Vincent. "You let him stay where he is, doctor. The money will be paid."

Before I could say anything, the door opens and in comes the dame that poses for all the magazine covers, dressed like a nurse. I never was much on describin'—I probably wouldn't have got ten people to watch the battle of Gettysburg if I'd have been the press agent—but this was the kind of dame that all the wealthy patients fall in love with in the movies—yeh, and out of 'em! The little white cap on top of her head looked like a dash of whipped cream on a peach sundae, and if you wouldn't have blowed up the city hall for the smile she sent around the room, I feel sorry for you. She crosses over and, in passin' me, she begs my pardon and threw that smile into high.

A hundred and fifty a week, eh? Well—I dives in my inside pocket.

"May I have your check, Mister—eh—ah—" pipes the doc.

"Green," I helps him out, "Johnny Green. Can you have a *check*? You said it!" I sits down and writes one out.

"Why this is for three hundred dollars!" he busts out, lookin' at it.

"Even so, brother," I grins, stealin' a slant at the Venus de California. "That's for me and the Kid. Gimme a room next to his and—"

"Do you think this is a hotel?" he frowns at me.

"I should care!" I tells him. "Let me in—that's all *I* want!"

With that the nurse remarks that the Kid is ready to see us, so me and Miss Vincent folleys her down the hall and she opens a door and calls in,

"Visitors, Mister Scanlan!"

"Yeh?" pipes the Kid in a show-em-the exit voice. "Ah— can I have a drink of—ah—water?"

"Certainly," she says. "I'll bring it now."

"Don't rush it!" says the Kid. "It might curdle! Wait till the attendance falls off a bit!"

She laughs—and Miss Vincent didn't.

"Oho!" whispers the pet of the movies. "Like that, eh?"

We go in the room, and there's Scanlan layin' in the whitest bed I even seen in my life and lookin' about as miserable as a millionaire's nephew on the day his uncle dies. There's about three hundred pillows under his head and neck, his arm is all bandaged up and beside the bed is a table with a set of flowers on it.

And then there was that nurse!

"Pretty soft!" I says.

The Kid grins and then twists around to Miss Vincent and groans.

"Does it hurt much, you poor dear?" she says.

"I wonder how I stand it!" pipes the Kid, keepin' his face from me.

"Can I get you anything?" she asks him after a minute.

"Well," answers the Kid, "if I did want something we could send Johnny for it." He looks at me meanin'ly. "Go out and git the right time!" he tells me. "And while you're at it—take lots of it!"

I went outside and closed the door. I remembered bein' in a hospital once, where they was examinin' guys for nerves, and one of the tests was hittin' 'em in the knee with a book and watchin' if their legs flew out. I don't remember the name of the book, but I figured on takin' a chance. I breezed out to the desk in the hall and filled out one of them entry blanks about myself, and then I dug up the doctor.

"Doc," I says, "I wish you'd gimme the East and West, there's somethin' the matter with my nerve. I know you can fix me up, if anybody can, because you got so much yourself."

"Just what is the East and West?" he asks me.

"Why, look me over!" I explains. "I wanna see what I need or should get rid of."

He leads me in a little room to one side, and goes over me like a lawyer lookin' for a clause in a contract he can bust. He looks at my tongue till it begin to quiver from exposure to the air; he clocks my pulse at a mile, two miles and over the jumps; he stuck a telephone like you see in the foreign movies over my heart and listened in on the internal gossip for twenty minutes;

he walloped me on the chest with the best he had and made me sing a song called "Ah-ah-ah-ah-ah-ah-ah-ah!" Then he shakes his head and tells me to put on my coat.

"You're one of the healthiest specimens I ever examined!" he says. "There's absolutely nothing the matter with you."

"Well, that's certainly tough, doc," I tells him, "because I sure want to win one of them rooms like Scanlan has. I—wait a minute!" I hollers, gettin' a flash. "You didn't gimme the book test!"

I hops over to the desk and grabs up a book off it. It was a big thick one called "Paralysis to Pneumonia," and was written by a couple of Greeks named "Symptoms and Therapeutics." I never heard of the thing before, and I wished it had been "Uncle Tom's Cabin" or somethin' like that, but I took a chance.

"Here!" I says. "I don't know if this is the right one or not, but let's try it out on my knee, eh?"

I seen he didn't make me, so I explains about the nerve test I seen where some of the guys throwed out their legs when hit, and some of 'em didn't. He gimme the laugh then, and tells me to look out of the window. I did and they's a terrible crash in back of me, but I kept lookin' out like he told me. Then he says all right, I can turn around, and, when I did, I see the book case has fell over on the floor. He claims if I had been nervous, I would have jumped eighty feet when it crashed down and as they is nothin' the matter with me, I might as well be on my way. Well, I was up against it—but only for a minute. That last crack of his gimme an idea. I makes a leap across the floor, grabs my heart and starts to shake and shiver like a bum in one of them "Curse of Drink" productions.

"What's the matter?" he calls out.

I looks wildly around the room, and I seen a fly upside down on the window-sill tryin' to get to its feet.

"Oh!" I says. "I'm so nervous, doc, I'm shakin' like a crap-shooter. D'ye see that fly? Well, it must have fell off the window just then—it gimme an awful shock—y'know that sudden noise and—"

He throws up his hands.

"Come!" he tells me. "I'll assign you to a room."

That's how I come to get mixed up with the Red Cross.

Pretty soon they had the Kid's arm better than it ever was, but as they was still workin' on his nerves, we stuck around at the sanitarium. We're both on a diet, which meant that at each meal-time we was fed about enough food to nourish a healthy infant about a half hour old. The general idea of the stuff was along nursery lines, too—milk, eggs and baby fodder, three times a day. I was O.K. when I went in there, but in a couple of weeks I was the prize patient on account of them meals. They tell me I raved one night and bellered for a rattle, and Scanlan made the nurse tell him all about Jack the Giant Killer and Old Mother Hubbard. The place must have been run by a guy who believed in lettin' the dumb animals live, because you couldn't have got a piece of meat in there, if you begged 'em for it till you was black in the face. You could have milk and eggs or eggs and milk—that was the limit!

One mornin' the orderly forgets himself and asks me what I want for breakfast. I thought they had let down the bars at last, and I all but jumped out of the bed.

"Gimme a steak, French fried potatoes, coffee and hot rolls," I says. "Have the potatoes well done and the steak rare."

"Rave on," he answers me. "Do you want the eggs boiled, fried or scrambled? Ain't there no particular way you like 'em?"

"Not no more!" I groans, and falls back on the sheets.

The only bright spot in the whole thing was Miss Woods, the nurse that caused me to enter the place. She used to come in every mornin' and make me play a thermometer was a lollypop and I held the thing in my mouth while she took my temperature and pulled a clock on my pulse. Then the orderly would come in and take the fruit friends had left for me, and I'd be all set for the day. When I kicked about the food, Miss Woods claimed I ought to be tickled to get eggs to eat, because they was very expensive on account of the late war. I says I didn't know they had been fightin' with eggs in Europe, and she laughs and says I'm delicious. She brought me in a book to read and on the cover it's all about the nights of Columbus. I didn't even open the thing, because what kind of nights could Columbus have had—they was nothin' doin' in them days. She asks me what my occupation was and says maybe she could arrange so's I could work at it while I was there to keep my mind off things. I says I *dared* anything to keep my mind off of her, and she kinda frowns; so's to brighten things up I says before I come there I had been a deck steward on a submarine, and it gets a laugh. Then she says I looked like a bookkeeper, and I didn't know whether that was a boost or a knock, so I passed it off by sayin' I had a chance to be that when young, but had to give it up because I couldn't stand the smell of ink.

After we have kidded like that for a while, I admits bein' Kid Scanlan's manager, and with that she suddenly runs to the door and closes it tight. She comes back on tip-toes, leans over the bed lookin' at me for a minute and then she asks me very soft would I do somethin' for her. I had got as far as offerin' to dive off the Singer Buildin' into a bucket of water, when she cuts me off and tells me to listen to her as they wasn't much time.

She asked me had I ever noticed a big, husky, black-haired guy out in the exercise yard. I said I had. I remembered a big whale of a man, with the face of a frightened kid, walkin' up and down, up and down, all day long. Every now and then he'd stop and pick up a pebble or a handful of dirt and take it to one side where he'd examine it for half an hour. Then he'd throw it away and start that sentry thing again.

Well, she said, this bird had been down to South America where he had discovered some kind of a mineral that had made him very rich and some kind of a fever that had made him very sick. He was at the sanitarium so's the doctors could keep a eye on him, the bettin' bein' about seven to five that he would go nutty, if some excavatin' wasn't done immediately on his dome. A operation will save him, but his parents won't think of it, and there you are. When she stopped, I told her that whilst I never had performed no operations before, beyond once when I pulled a loose tooth of Scanlan's between the second and third round of a fight, I would get somebody to sneak me in some tools and get to work on the big guy the first chance I got. She give a little squeal and says that wasn't what she wanted me to do, gettin' pale and prettier every minute. I seen I pulled a bone, so I asks her to come right out with it and whatever she said I'd do it or break a leg.

"Then when Mr. Scanlan takes his exercise every day with the boxing gloves and punching bag," she says, "get him to persuade Arthur to join him. Arthur would do it for him quicker than he would for me or any of the doctors. He thinks we are all in league against him and he admires Mr. Scanlan—I've read it in his face as he watches him out in the yard. Arthur himself was a noted athlete before he went to South America. He might even box with Mr. Scanlan. That would lessen the tension on his mind and we might get him to see that an operation is—Oh! Will you do it?" she breaks off suddenly, grabbin' my hand.

"Will I?" I says, holdin' on to that hand. "If Scanlan don't box him, I'll take him on myself!"

"Oh, thank you—thank you!" she whispers, "I—"

"That's all right!" I cuts her off. "Is—ah—is the big fellow any relation to you?"

She blushed. Yeh—and I looked at her, forgettin' a lot of things about both of us that didn't quite match—and wished! I got everything I had together for one good try, bein' handicapped by the fact that I still had her hand and that room was goin' around like a top. And then, poor boob—I looked down at the hand I didn't have, wonderin' why she didn't answer me—and saw the answer on one finger. The darned cold, glitterin' thing seemed to sneer at me. I felt like I'd stopped one with my chin, and somethin' went outa me that ain't back yet. What? Well, a guy can hope, can't he?

Say! That ring must have cost five hundred bucks—it was a pip!

I grabbed a drink of that darned milk to steady myself, and I seen from the way she looked at me that she got me.

"I see!" I says, lettin' go of the hand that belonged to friend Arthur. "He—and he went to South America, eh?"

"Listen!" she whispers, bendin' over. "You know now what this means to me. If you'll help me, I'll do anything for you! Why—"

I sat up in bed and grabbed her hand again.

"Anything?" I asks her.

She looks out the window, gets pale and grits her teeth. You could see she wished she hadn't said it, but she was game and was standin' pat.

"Anything!" she says.

"Then for the love of heaven!" I shoots out, "get me a piece of meat! This egg and milk thing is drivin' me nutty!"

She wheeled around so quick the scared look was still on her face, and for a minute we both just looked. Then she give a kinda nervous little laugh, grabbed both my hands, squeezed 'em like a man—and blew!

Oh, boy! I ain't no hard loser but—

Well, it wasn't no trick at all to get big Arthur to box with the Kid. He took to it like a chorus girl does to a telephone and what puzzled me was why none of them fifty dollar doctors hadn't thought of it before. I guess it was because they was nobody there husky enough to handle him by themselves, because Arthur packed a wallop in each hand that meant curtains, if it landed. Behind that was six-foot-two of bone and about two hundred and forty pounds of muscle.

The Kid labored with him like a mother with a baby. He taught him how to duck, feint, jab, uppercut, swing, stall, rough in the clinches, everything he knew, and Arthur learned awful quick. So quick that we had to cut the bouts down to twenty minutes each, because the big guy didn't *know* and he was *tryin'* with every punch!

The doctors told Scanlan to talk operation to him, and the Kid tried it once. Arthur stopped boxin' and looked at him so reproachful that Scanlan refused to mention it again. He said he looked just like a kid that come down Christmas mornin' and found no tree.

Finally, me and the Kid packed up and kissed the sanitarium good-by, but every afternoon at three we went over and Scanlan put on the gloves with Arthur for a while, because I had give my word to his girl. Arthur got so he lived all the rest of the day and night lookin' forward to three o'clock in the afternoon. He snarled at the doctors, cuffed the orderlies, didn't know Miss Woods from the iron gate that kept him in there, but the minute Scanlan breezed into the yard with the gloves his face would be one big smile.

This went on for three months—and then Miss Vincent stepped into the thing.

She wanted to know where the Kid was goin' every afternoon at three o'clock, and like a simp, I told her the whole story. She thanks me with a odd look that I didn't get till that night, when the Kid comes tearin' in to our room at the hotel and slams the door. When he gets where he can make his tongue do like he asks it, he says it's all off between him and Miss Vincent. By usin' some judgment and four hours of time I find out that Miss Vincent thinks this stuff about the Kid boxin' Arthur is a lot of bunk and the Kid was really goin' back to the sanitarium every day to see Miss Woods. She has give that nurse the once over and then used some woman's arithmetic which makes two and two equal nine, get me? Well, one word led to another, and finally she tells him if he don't cut the sanitarium out, she's off him for life.

That's a bad way to handle Scanlan. He's Irish and—you know!

He told her we give our word and he was gonna box Arthur till they remodeled Arthur's skull, no matter what happened. Then Miss Vincent gets sensible and weeps. In a minute the Kid is on his knees, and she shows more sense than usual by chasin' him at that point. At the bottom of the stairs, Scanlan calls up and asks if he can kiss her good night. She tells him it's too late now, he has missed the psychological moment.

That last was what had the Kid up in the air. He didn't know what it meant, except that it was a cinch she wasn't wishin' him good luck. That psychological thing was past me, too. I looked it up in the dictionary, and it was there all right, but it could have been in Russia as far as I was concerned, because the way it described it was over my head. The Kid finally puts it right up to Miss Vincent, and she tells him to find out for himself.

"Go over to that trick sanitarium of yours, and ask Miss Woods," she tells him scornfully. "Maybe *she* can tell you what it means!"

But at two o'clock, when the Kid is leavin' for his daily maulin' bee with big Arthur, she comes along in her racin' car and asks him to go to Los Angeles with her. The Kid stalls and says he's just about got time to get over and give the South American entry a workout, although he'd rather take the ride with her than defend his title against a one-armed blind man. She frowns for a minute, and then she smiles and says hop in with her and she'll drive him over to the sanitarium.

When they blowed in that night at seven o'clock, I seen the Kid looks kinda worried, while he's washin' the Golden West off his face and neck, so I ask him how Arthur is comin' along. Scanlan coughs a couple of times and then he says he don't know, because he wasn't able to get over there that afternoon—the first he'd missed since I promised the world's champion girl I'd assist her. While I'm still bawlin' him out, he claims it wasn't his fault, because the car broke down in the middle of California and they had to get towed back.

I *will* say I was sorry to find out that Miss Vincent wasn't above a little rough stuff! Oh, you ladies!

The next day Genaro suddenly decides to take a scene in the Kid's movie, and as we was under contract we had to stay. The third afternoon, Miss Vincent gets a terrible headache and the Kid has to sit on the hotel porch with her, readin' out loud her press notices from the movie magazines.

I kept out of it, but thinkin' about Arthur and that little nurse over there had me bitin' nails, and the next day I told the Kid if he didn't go out and trade wallops with Arthur, I was through as his pilot. I said that right out loud in front of Miss Vincent, lookin' her right in them famous baby-blue eyes of hers. But you can't figure women—she crossed me and tells the Kid to go and she'd go with him!

We went out in her racin' car, with me ridin' on the runnin' board and thinkin' what a fine thing accident insurance was for a guy of moderate means. By dumb luck we missed crashin' into the scenery along the road and stopped outside the iron gates of the sanitarium. We had hardly got in the office, when from down the hall we heard what sounded like a race riot, and a couple of orderlies goes past us so fast that I didn't believe it could be done, although I seen 'em. The Kid runs down to where the noise was comin' from and I tagged along in the rear, stoppin' with him outside a big two-doored room, where from the sounds that crashed out from inside they was puttin' on a dress rehearsal of a race riot.

While we stood there lookin' at each other, a familiar deep snarlin' voice roars out over the others—they was a scream, too, that made me neck and neck with the Kid as we busted in the locked doors and went sprawlin' inside.

Oh, boy!

A half dozen nurses and two or three doctors is lined up against the wall on the far side, crouchin' back of an operatic table and tryin' to force their bodies through the hard cement. The place looks like a cyclone had hit it, with the walls scraped and scarred and the floor covered with plaster and what not like the show-room of a junk shop. Half on the floor and half on a chair is Miss Woods. I hoped she had only fainted.

In the middle of the room and backin' against the doors is a big, growlin', red-eyed killer that used to be Arthur.

Most of his clothes is torn off where some of them poor little human bein's had tried to hold him, and over his head he's swingin' a iron pole he'd torn from the fancy front gate outside. Each time he swings, he comes nearer that bunch with nothin' between them and Heaven but a white enameled table. He didn't seem to notice Scanlan, who slid almost to his feet, and rightin' himself like a cat, stepped back to size the thing up. Then with a growl, Arthur chops at the operatin' table with the pole and crumbles it like a berry box. The women screamed—I think one of 'em fainted. The doctors spread in front of them, as Arthur raised the pole to finish the job.

And then Scanlan, poppin' up from somewheres, jumps in front of Arthur, his face the color of that busted table, but his body as steady as the Rockies, as he plants himself there before the big guy, swingin' his head back easily before that tremblin' iron pole. The Kid throws his hands up in a fightin' position and dances from one foot to the other lookin' for a openin', like a guy with a pail of water tryin' to put out hell! Arthur hesitates, starin' wildly at the Kid, and then his face begins to change till it's almost human. He looks like he's tryin' to think.

"Come on!" bawls Scanlan—loud, to keep the crack out of his voice. "Come on!" He dances around Arthur and makes a pass at him. "I got some new ones to show you to-day!" he yells. "Hurry up, or we—won't—have—time—to—mix it!"

I remember the head doc told me afterwards it was because the big feller had been doin' that every day—boxin' with the Kid—for so long that it—

But what's that matter now? Arthur dropped that iron pole, put up his hands, grins like a baby and rocks the Kid with a straight left, while them nurses and doctors tumbled out of the room thankin' their different gods. Somebody carried out Miss Woods, too.

I guess Scanlan never battled before like he did in the next ten minutes, because he was fightin' for the biggest purse he ever climbed in a ring for—his life! The big guy smashed him all over the place tryin' for a knockout like the Kid had taught him, crushin' his ribs in the clinches till Scanlan's breathin' cut me to the heart and rainin' wallops on him like a machine gun. Me? Oh, I didn't do much but root for the Kid. Y'see I was beside that operatic table when Arthur lammed it with the pole—some of it kinda glanced off and I stopped it with my head. A game little bantam of a doctor hopped around 'em, as they slewed over the floor, lookin' like a referee—but he was simply tryin' to slip friend Arthur a hypodermic while Scanlan kept him busy.

Finally, the Kid staggers Arthur with a lucky right smash to the chin, and then a half a dozen left and rights to the body cut his size down to where the Kid could put all he had left in one swing—and it's all over. The little doc with the hypo gets busy, and, when we left the room, Arthur was headed for the operatin' pen—his trip havin' been interrupted by the slight excitement Scanlan had stopped!

Well, me and the Kid was hustled upstairs to be fussed over, windin' up, you might say, where we started, in the hospital. After a time Miss Woods comes up and thanks us—at least she made a stab at it and weeps. The operation had been a success, and when Arthur could walk he was gonna reward Miss Woods for her lovin' care by marryin' her, and she looked like she thought that was enough—ain't women a scream?

We was talkin' to the doctor, when Miss Vincent come in —stands in the doorway for a minute lookin' like a swell picture in a punk frame, and comes to the Kid with a yours-for-keeps look in her eyes. Scanlan throws up his head like he's just thought of somethin'.

"Say!" he pipes through the bandages. "I know what that psychological moment thing is now—the doc has just been tellin' me. It seems," he says with a grin. "It seems I pulled one off here this afternoon!"

THE END

Lightning Source UK Ltd.
Milton Keynes UK
UKHW021944280519
343492UK00005B/151/P

9 781388 317744